"You're Telling Me That You're Saving Yourself For Marriage? That's The Oldest Trick In The Book."

"I told you that you wouldn't understand. I'll leave in the morning," she said and turned away from him to walk back to the house. She crossed her arms over her chest, feeling the impending crush of defeat. Holding off on sex had been a calculated risk, but Calista had suspected that it would be difficult to motivate Leo to marry her quickly unless she waited until they married.

Three seconds later, she felt her hand caught by his. "Not so fast," he said.

She stopped in surprise, searching his face.

"The least you can do is give me a chance to change your mind. Or see if you can change mine," he said.

"I just think I'm one of those women who jump all the way into the pool of commitment. I totally understand if you're not looking for that. Most men aren't."

"I'm not most men," he said.

Dear Reader,

I'm so excited to share Leo's story with you. He's the missing piece to the Medici brother puzzle! Leo lost even more than his brothers. He's had so much to overcome. Can reuniting with his brothers help make him whole again? Can marrying a woman with excellent breeding clean up his image? Or maybe, despite her own secrets, she can inspire him to be the man he's always wanted to be.

I hope you've enjoyed the journey the Medici brothers took to reconnect with each other and find true love. I have truly loved writing their stories and wish you your own love to last a lifetime.

Want to write me about the Medici brothers or any of my other books? I love to hear from readers. I can be reached at leanne@leannebanks.com and you can learn more about me and my books at www.leannebanks.com.

Best wishes,

Leanne Banks

LEANNE BANKS

SECRETS OF THE PLAYBOY'S BRIDE

Silhouette®
Desire

Published by Silhouette Books

America's Publisher of Contemporary Romance

SILHOUETTE BOOKS

ISBN-13: 978-0-373-73015-5

SECRETS OF THE PLAYBOY'S BRIDE

Copyright © 2010 by Leanne Banks

Recycling programs
for this product may
not exist in your area.

Visit Silhouette Books at www.eHarlequin.com

Printed in U.S.A.

LEANNE BANKS

is a *New York Times* and *USA TODAY* bestselling author who is surprised every time she realizes how many books she has written. Leanne loves chocolate, the beach and new adventures. To name a few, Leanne has ridden on an elephant, stood on an ostrich egg (no, it didn't break), gone parasailing and indoor skydiving. Leanne loves writing romance because she believes in the power and magic of love. She lives in Virginia with her family and four-and-a-half-pound Pomeranian named Bijou. Visit her Web site at www.leannebanks.com.

This book is dedicated to my Silhouette Desire buddies: Rachel Bailey, Maya Banks, Jules Bennett, Jan Colley, Yvonne Lindsay, Emily McKay, Charlene Sands and Maxine Sullivan. Thank you for getting me through!

One

Leonardo Grant caught the woman in his arms, absorbing her feminine impact and taking in swinging blond hair and seductive curves just before he felt something cold and wet slide down his chest.

"Oops," the blond woman said with a contrite expression, glancing from her nearly empty glass to his shirt. "I'm so sorry," she said. "I'm not usually such a klutz. I just wasn't watching where I was going. Let me get a napkin for you."

Despite the spill, the woman *emanated* class. No surprise, given she was attending one of Philadelphia's most exclusive charity events. He wondered who her date was. A woman this beautiful wouldn't have arrived alone. "No problem," he said smoothly. "I can get my own napkin."

"But I feel terrible. And you probably feel worse in that soggy shirt," she said motioning toward a waiter.

Charmed by how flustered she was, Leo allowed her to fuss over him for a moment while he studied her from head to toe. Silky shoulder-length blond hair framed an oval face with wide green eyes, a pert nose and a mobile, sensual mouth. He glanced lower, taking in her lean but curvy body. She worked out, he observed, taking in the slight muscle in her biceps. Her strapless dress revealed the tops of her creamy breasts and a narrow waist. The slit in her full-length gown gave him a peek at shapely legs.

A furrow formed beneath her brow as she mopped at his chest. "Maybe we could find you another shirt," she said.

Leo bit back a chuckle. He could have a shirt delivered to him in five minutes, but she was so much more interesting. "I can stand it," he said. "But we should replace your drink."

"I don't know," she said, full of doubt. "Maybe dumping my margarita on your shirt is a sign for me to stop even though that was my first one for the evening," she said.

He shrugged. "If at first you don't succeed," he said and extended his hand. "Leo Grant."

"Calista," she said, sliding her smooth, well-manicured hand in his. "Calista French. You've been such a good sport. I truly am sorry."

Her last name tripped a trigger, and Leo searched his memory for details. There'd been so many names over the years, names of people his guardian had tricked and used. Once Leo had run away, he'd tried to forget them all. He pushed the thought aside. "No more apologies necessary. You rescued me from boredom."

She held his gaze for an extra few seconds. "You don't seem the type of man to allow boredom."

He felt a flicker of sensual awareness snap between them. "I don't," he said. "I wasn't planning on staying long tonight anyway."

"Lucky guy," she said in a low, conspiratorial voice. "I'm a member of the group who sponsored the event, so I can't duck out until at least half-time. The only thing that makes it bearable is I really believe in the cause we're supporting this year. Support for Abused Children. A close second to that cause in my opinion is the mentoring program for inner-city youth."

"Are you a mentor?" he asked, surprised that a classy bombshell like her would spend her spare time with needy youth.

"Of course," she said, then shot him a look of sexy challenge. "Aren't you?"

"I could be," he said. "Maybe you could tell me more about the program sometime over drinks or dinner." He pulled a card from his pocket and pressed it into her hand.

Biting her lip, she searched his face. "I can have the program director give you a call. She's more knowledgeable about specific needs than I am."

"Are your turning down my invitation for dinner?" he asked.

She cleared her throat, but didn't fidget. "I was taught that a woman never makes the first call. Especially if she's spilled a margarita on the man. I should go. It's been a pleasure."

He watched her walk away, appreciating the curve of her backside. So, she didn't want to make the first move. He had no problem stepping up. Even though she'd neglected to give him her phone number, he could have it within minutes. He'd make a request now, he thought, reaching for his BlackBerry. Calista French stimulated his curiosity. When it came to women, Leo always got what he wanted. Unfortunately, once they discovered the extent of his wealth, women tended to fall over themselves to please him. At that point, he quickly became bored, but Calista intrigued him. Aside from her obvious assets, he'd liked the sound of her laughter and the sparkle in her eye. He'd been working nonstop lately. He could use a distraction, and she didn't seem the type to be overly impressed by his money. She oozed good breeding—something he certainly lacked. In the back of his mind, Leo was always looking for the perfect woman to make him *clean*.

Calista's heart pounded as she walked away from one of the wealthiest men in the world. Drawing in a calming breath, she accepted the bottle of water the waiter offered on her way to the opposite end of the grand ballroom. She rarely drank alcohol because she always had to be on guard. Since her father had died, there'd always been too much at stake.

Time would tell her if her fishing expedition with Leonardo Grant was successful. He was the kind of man who liked a challenge, and she had spent the last two months planning how to become *his* challenge. He was better looking in person than in the rare photographs she'd seen in the newspaper. Tall with dark hair and black eyes, he had a dangerous air that seemed to whisper beneath the surface.

She knew he was a huge benefactor of charitable causes. Probably paying his own version of penance for what his father had done, she thought bitterly. Not many people knew Leo Grant was the son of the late, unlamented Clyde Hawkins. Leo might have had enough money to pay for most of his past to go away, but she had a photograph of Clyde Hawkins and the boy who'd ruined her father. The boy in the photo was Leo Grant and he didn't know it, but he was going to help her.

On Sunday afternoon, Calista pulled her eight-year-old, but well-maintained, BMW in front of her cousin Sharon's home in the suburbs just as she did every week. Two hours from Philadelphia, the home had mostly insulated her twin sisters from the scandal that had wreaked havoc on their lives years ago.

Calista smiled at the beautifully-tended shrubs and flowers. Even with a son of their own, Sharon and her husband, Walter, had tended her sisters in the same loving way they approached everything. She walked up the steps to the small cottage and knocked on the door. "Hello? Anyone home?"

She heard a screech followed by pounding feet. The door flew open and her sister Tina and Sharon's son, Justin, elbowed each other. "Beat ya," Tina said and gave Calista a hug.

"Uh-uh," Justin said. "I got here first."

Despite the fact that Tina was seventeen and Justin was nearly fifteen, the two engaged in friendly competition at every opportunity.

Her other sister Tami appeared behind them with more predictable teenage cool. "As if it matters who gets there first," Tami said, yawning as she nudged past them. "Cal, can you take me for a mani-pedi? My nails are a mess."

"I wanted to ride go-karts," Tina said.

"Second that one," Justin said. "I'd win again."

Tami rolled her eyes. "Tina always gets her way. I'll watch."

"Maybe we could do both," Calista said. "Go-karts first, then a mani or pedi."

"I can't sit still long enough for a manicure, but I'll take the pedicure," Tina said.

"And you can just let me off at the ice-cream parlor," Justin said. "It's on the way."

Sharon appeared in the doorway and smiled. "Cal, sweetie, I didn't know you were here."

Calista reached forward to embrace her cousin. "I barely had time to knock with these two," she said.

Sharon ruffled her son's hair. "I shouldn't be surprised. What's the sister outing for today?" she asked.

"Looks like go-karts and a manicure," Calista said.

"What a combination," Sharon said. "Can I chat with you before you go?"

"Sure," Calista said, stepping inside the house. "And Justin can join us."

"For a manicure?" Sharon said.

"Go-karts and ice cream," Justin said.

"Hmm. We'll see," Sharon said and led Calista to the back porch. "Would you like something to drink?"

Calista shook her head. "I'm fine. What's up?"

"It's Tami," Sharon said quietly. "I caught her smoking again and I don't like the crowd she's hanging around. She got in well past her curfew last night and I think I smelled alcohol on her breath."

Calista's stomach clenched. It had been her most fervent goal for her sisters to grow up in a safe, nurturing environment until it was time for them to go to college. Since Sharon was a stay-at-home mom, and her husband, Walter, made a modest income, Calista provided all the necessary financial support for her sisters since she'd finished college three years ago.

Now, with both her sisters graduating from high school, Calista was determined that they would attend the college of their choice, regardless of the expense. There was also the added complication of Tami's asthma. Even with insurance, the cost of her medications and treatments had prevented Calista from being able to save extra money for her sisters' future.

"I'll talk to her," Calista said. "I know stepping up to parent my sisters hasn't been easy."

"Walter and I love them. We just wish we could better afford them," Sharon said wryly. "But I knew when I married a carpenter I wasn't destined for a life of luxury."

"I think you got a good deal. You got a life of love. That's more than many of us will ever see," Calista said, knowing a life of love wasn't likely in her own future. She couldn't imagine trusting anyone enough to let down her guard. Look what had happened to her mother, Calista and her sisters when they'd counted on her father.

"Speaking of love life, I can't believe no men have been asking you out," Sharon said.

"I may have met someone special recently," she said, laying the groundwork for the rest of her plan. "Time will tell."

"Oh, surely you can cough up more than that," Sharon said. "Is he kind? Funny? Gorgeous?"

She smiled at her cousin's priorities. Wealth hadn't even made the list. "It's too soon. I don't want to jinx it."

Hours later, after go-karts, a pedicure for Tami and Tina and ice cream for all, Calista snagged her sister Tami before she disappeared into the house. "Hey, what's the rush?" she asked, grabbing her sister's hand. "Sit here on the porch with me before I have to go."

"Graham is supposed to call," Tami said, speaking of her latest boyfriend.

"You can talk to him after I leave," Calista said.

"If Sharon lets me," Tami muttered, tossing her multicolored bangs from her eyes. "Honestly, I'm going to be eighteen in August, but the way she treats me, I may as well be in preschool."

"Slight exaggeration," Calista said in a dry tone she couldn't conceal.

Tami slid a rebellious sideways glance at her.

"August will be here before you know it and you'll be off to college."

"Freedom at last," Tami said.

"I hate to remind you, but college means more studying than ever," Calista said, then waved her hand to dismiss the subject. "How are things going for you lately?" she asked.

Tami regarded her suspiciously. "Sharon told you, didn't she?"

"Told me what?"

Tami sighed and glanced away. "She caught me smoking. I begged her not to say anything to you."

"Why?" Calista asked, her heart twisting. "I thought you and I were closer than that."

"We are," Tami said, fiddling with her hair. "I just didn't want you to be mad at me."

"I'm not mad. I'm worried. You know you have asthma, so you shouldn't stress your lungs by smoking. I just want you to be safe and happy." Calista gathered her sister into her arms. "That's all I've ever wanted for you."

"It was just once," Tami said and closed her eyes. "I've been thinking about Mom lately. I wish she hadn't died."

"I do too," Calista said, pulling back slightly and looking into her sister's eyes. "But we've got each other. Don't you forget that. If you need anything, anytime, give me a call. Just promise me you'll be safe."

"Promise," she said. "Prom is two weeks away. Are you still going to take us shopping for dresses next Saturday?"

"Wouldn't miss it," Calista said.

During the drive back to Philadelphia, she worried about her sister. Tami and Tina possessed diametrically opposed personalities. Tina was easygoing in her personal life, but competitive and intense with sports and grades. She would be eligible for scholarships and aid, but more money would be needed. Tami was intense about her personal relationships and had to be pushed to focus on academics. Fortunately, both her sisters were naturally intelligent and had been accepted at the colleges of their choice. Now, all Calista had to do was come up with hundreds of thousands of dollars to make it happen for them.

Leo glanced at the background information on Calista French for the third time. She hadn't lied. She was a card-carrying member of the exclusive women's society who'd sponsored the charity benefit, had graduated with honors from a top Ivy League university, was currently employed as an analyst for an insurance company and was active in local charities. Her mother and father were dead; her two sisters lived a couple hours away.

Her background was unblemished with the exception of her father's financial failure and subsequent death. Apparently her father was a terrible money manager;

however, Leo vaguely remembered that Clyde had pulled something over on a man with the last name French.

Another skeleton, he thought, gritting his teeth. He glanced at the photograph of Calista and remembered her smile and breathless laughter. Damn it, she made him curious. It might not be wise to pursue a woman whose life had been negatively affected by his pseudoguardian, but Leo was more tired than ever of being bound by his past. He picked up the phone and dialed her cell number.

"Hello?" she asked and her voice felt as if it seeped inside him like honey.

"Hi. Leo Grant. You said you couldn't make the first call," he said. "So I'm making it."

He heard the soft intake of her breath. "What a surprise. How did you get my number?"

"I have ways. Do you mind?"

She paused, a half beat that put him on edge. "No, I don't."

He grinned at the odd thrill that raced through him. "Good. Dinner tonight at Antoine's at seven. I'll have my driver pick you up wherever you say."

"I'm sorry. I can't tonight."

Unaccustomed to being refused, he felt a twist of irritation. "Tomorrow night?"

"I would like that," she said. "But there's no need for you to send a car. I can drive myself."

Calista hung up the phone and mentally checked step two off her list. The following afternoon, a last-minute meeting at work nearly made her late, but she rushed to pull herself together. Thank goodness for all the charm school classes her mother had required her to take. At the time, they'd seemed dreadfully old-fashioned, but now she was thankful to know how to present a calm face even when she didn't feel that way.

She strode into Antoine's and asked the maître d' to direct her to Leo's table. The man nodded. "Your dinner partner is at the bar," he said.

Glancing up to find Leo staring at her, she felt a dip in her stomach. No doubt about it, the man was as gorgeous as sin, but it was the intense way he looked at her that affected her. There was a hard-won strength about him that appealed to her despite the fact that she hated his father for what he'd done to her family. She smiled as he walked toward her. "Hello again," she said.

"Are you hungry?" he asked as the maître d' led them to a table in the corner next to the window.

"I will be as soon as I catch my breath," she said.

"Busy day?" he asked.

She nodded. "And always a minicrisis at the end of the day. How about you?"

"I just negotiated a new deal with a company in China. That will keep us busy for a while. Would you like something to drink? Don't I owe you a margarita?" he suggested with just a hint of sensual mischief in his eyes.

She laughed. "Thank you. I'll stick with one glass of wine tonight. What kind of business are you in?" she asked, even though she already knew quite a bit about Leo. She'd made it her mission to know as much about him as possible—even the kind of women he favored. She'd been pleased to learn he tended toward well-bred, well-educated blondes. Nice that she didn't have to dye her hair, she thought.

"Shipping and transportation," he said.

"And international since you just mentioned China," she said.

He nodded. "It's a must with the global economy. What about you?"

"I'm an analyst for Collier Associates. It's not my first love, but I have a great boss."

"What's your first love?" he asked and she noticed his voice had a caressing quality to it. She could almost feel it on her skin.

"I love astronomy, but now that I've worked for a couple years, I've decided it's better to enjoy that as a hobby," she said.

"So you like to study the stars," he said. "Interesting. How long have you had your head in the upper atmosphere?"

She smiled at his teasing tone. "Close to forever. I asked for a telescope when I was a very young child. A lot of kids get them, then they're abandoned in the attic. You strike me as the kind of man with both feet on the ground. Do you remember what you did with your telescope?"

"I didn't ever have a telescope," he said, with a chuckle that didn't meet his eyes. "I didn't have a childhood."

She blinked at his statement. "What? Everyone has a childhood. Unless you were hatched or are an alien."

He shook his head. "As far as I'm concerned, life for me began at sixteen. But enough about my boring past. I'd like to know more about you."

He was more charming than she'd planned, but she supposed she should have expected that. After all, he'd essentially been a grifter, a con artist. Wasn't that the job requirement for con artists?

Just after the server delivered their drinks, a man approached the table. He looked vaguely familiar to Calista, but she couldn't name him. She wondered if he was one of Leo's acquaintances, except he kept looking at her.

"Calista French. All grown up. I remember you as a young teen," the man said.

Calista searched the man's face but still couldn't recall him. "I'm sorry. I'm drawing a blank."

The man laughed but his eyes were cold. "William Barrett. I was one of your father's business partners."

Calista felt her blood drain to her feet. William Barrett had sued her father's estate and then gone after her mother after her father had died. She mustered a blank expression. "You're correct. I was very young. I hope you're enjoying your dinner. It's a lovely restaurant, isn't it?"

"Yes, it is. How is your mother these days?" he asked.

She couldn't quite keep from digging her fingernails into her palms, but at least her hands were in her lap out of sight. "My mother passed away several years ago."

Barrett raised his eyebrows. "Oh, I'm sorry. Of course, I knew about your father, but—"

The maître d' approached Barrett. "Sir, I've been asked by the manager to inform you that your party will receive a complimentary appetizer. We just need to know your preference. Your server has a menu at your table."

Barrett gave a loud bark of a laugh. "Must be my lucky day. Hope to see you again, Calista."

Calista said nothing and reached for her glass of wine, barely resisting the urge to hiss at the man.

"You don't like him, do you?" Leo asked.

"Was I so obvious?"

"You turned pale," he said.

"He treated my family poorly during a difficult time," she said.

"Then I'll tell his server to pour red wine on him," he said.

His suggestion lightened her mood. "Oh, they wouldn't do that on purpose," she said, feeling a slight pinch at the memory of the margarita she'd poured on Leo.

He lifted an eyebrow. "My personal assistant usually runs interference when I'm eating in a public place, but I allowed this man to approach because he might have been a friend of yours. Next time we're in public, I'll stick to my routine."

Although Calista had been raised in a relatively wealthy home, she'd never heard of her father employing an assistant for such a task. She glanced around. "Is your assistant here tonight?"

He nodded behind her and waved his hand. A brawny middle-aged man approached them. "George, this is Miss French. We'd prefer no interruptions for the remainder of the meal."

"Miss French," George said in a gruff voice with a nod.

"George, it's nice to meet you," Calista said, extending her hand.

Looking slightly uncomfortable, he shook her hand. "Pleasure to meet you also, Miss," he said then turned to Leo. "Enjoy your dinner, sir."

George turned around with his hands folded behind his back, creating a barrier between their table and the rest of the room.

Calista let out a sigh of relief. Barrett wouldn't be approaching her again that evening. "Must ask. What does he say to people who try to approach the table?"

"Mr. Grant and his guest would like to enjoy their meal

without interruption. Thank you for your consideration," he recited.

"Has it ever not worked?" she asked. "What happens if they ignore him?"

"That's only happened three times. George says, *I insist.*"

"And if that doesn't work?"

He hesitated, then smiled. "You want to know about the one time that a man wouldn't take no for an answer? George is a former boxer, but he was homeless when I met him. He's my trainer and sparring partner."

Surprised, she stared at him for a moment. "Is he your bodyguard?"

Leo laughed. "Hell, no. He's the best friend I've ever had. I just had to find a way to get him off the streets and the only way I could do it was to employ him. Shocked?"

"Yes." She paused a second. "In a good way."

He lifted his glass and clinked it against hers. "To no more interruptions."

A couple hours later, Leo escorted her downstairs and outside. He was tall and moved with athletic grace. He oozed confidence, strength and mystery even though she knew his secret. Sliding his fingers through hers, he looked down at her. "Come to my house for an after-dinner drink," he said, his eyes full of invitation.

Her stomach dipped, taking her by surprise. "I can't. I have my car," she said.

"One of my drivers can pick it up for you," he countered.

She was stunned at the heat that rushed through her. "I have to go to work tomorrow," she said and suddenly remembered she was supposed to be seducing him. "Rain check?"

He leaned toward her and pressed his mouth against hers. Her breath left her body.

"Yeah," he said. "I'll walk you to your car."

She vacillated, not wanting him to see her older vehicle. "Um."

"I insist," he said and slid his hand behind her back.

They passed a homeless man on the sidewalk with a can for donations. She watched in amazement as Leo stuffed a twenty dollar bill inside. "Take care," he murmured to the man.

"Thank you," the homeless man said. "Go in peace."

Leo glanced at her and must have read the surprise on her face. "In different circumstances, that could be me," he said.

Something in his tone jerked at her heart. He spoke as if he had insider experience. She slid another assessing glance at him. Who was this man? He was different than she'd expected.

They arrived at her car in the parking garage and a black Town Car pulled alongside them. "Don't worry. It's just George. He's also one of my drivers," he said. "Are you sure I can't persuade you to extend the evening?"

"You probably could," she said, surprised at the breathlessness in her voice. She had a plan here, a strategy. She shouldn't be this attracted to him. "But I'm hoping to appeal to your better nature and that you'll encourage me to get the rest I need for my busy workday tomorrow."

Leo gave a rough chuckle. "My better nature? I'm not sure that exists." He lowered his head and pressed his mouth against hers. His mouth was both firm and soft, exploring and seducing. "Come to my lake house this weekend," he muttered against her lips. "It will be your reward for being a good analyst."

Calista sighed. "I can't. I have a previous commitment on Saturday."

"Break it," he said.

"I really can't," she said. "I promised to take my younger sisters shopping for prom dresses on Saturday." She shot him a teasing smile. "Wanna join us? Your opportunity to get up close and personal with teen girl drama."

"Sounds tempting, but I'll pass," he said dryly. "Will you be done by Saturday evening?"

"Yes. Why?" she asked.

"Then we can leave for the lake on Saturday evening. We'll take my helicopter. Say yes," he said.

She looked into his deep brown eyes and felt a shudder of intuitive warning reverberate inside her. "Yes," she said and wondered if she was making a huge mistake.

"Good." He glanced down at her car and frowned. "You won't be driving this car home tonight."

"Why not?" she asked then noticed her tires had been slashed. Her stomach dipped. "Oh, no! Are all of them—"

Checking the tires on the other side of the car, he nodded. "All four." He glanced at the car next to hers. "Look," he said. "All the tires of the cars in this row have been slashed. Damn vandals," he muttered and waved for George to approach.

Calista mentally added up the cost of replacing the tires and stifled a groan. She had neither the time nor the money to spare for this.

"Yes, sir," George said to Leo.

"We're going to need to get Miss French's car towed to the garage so her tires can be replaced. Just use our garage."

"No, that's not necessary," she said.

"I insist," Leo said. "You can stay at my condo. It's just a few blocks from here."

Panic surged through her. "Oh, that's crazy. There's no reason I can't sleep at my own place tonight."

"Your vehicle won't be ready until the morning," he said, then shot her a half smile. "Don't worry. You won't be all alone with me. I have staff."

Two

Moments later, Leo dropped his Town Car with the valet, and they took an elevator to the penthouse of an exclusive condominium building. A woman greeted them at the door. "Good evening, Mr. Grant. Can I get something for you?"

"Would you like another glass of wine?" Leo asked as they entered. "Margarita?"

She shot him a sideways glance. "Just water please."

"Water for both of us, Brenda. Thank you," Leo said.

"This is very nice," she said, looking around at the posh furnishings.

"It works when I'm spending a lot of time in the city," he said with a shrug. "I have another place just outside of town where I rarely stay. This is convenient."

Brenda returned with chilled water. Calista gulped hers down.

"Are you upset about your tires?" he asked, studying her face.

"It's a little disturbing even though it wasn't personal," she said and realized a big part of the reason she wasn't more upset was because Leo had been there with her. She would have to be very careful around him. It would be all too easy to enjoy having a strong, decisive man on whom she could count and let her strategy slide from being her top priority. "I'm just thinking I need to get up early in the morning so I can go back to my apartment before work. I think I'm ready to turn in. Where is the guest room?"

"You have a choice of two beds. The guest bed, or mine," he said with an undertone of seduction.

She felt a quick rush of forbidden temptation but pushed the sensation aside. "I'm not sure I'd get much sleep in your bed," she admitted in a whisper. "And sleep is what I need."

He slid his finger over her jaw. "If you say so," he said, then lowered his head and kissed her.

The light scent of Calista's perfume lingered for a few seconds after she walked down the hallway to the guestroom. He inhaled deeply, wanting to catch the last bit of her. The taste of her was still on his lips, but he wanted more. He couldn't remember wanting a woman this much, this quickly. He wanted her in his bed tonight.

Calista was the flesh and blood equivalent of his dream woman. Classy, well-educated, polished, yet warm, she could make him clean. With her by his side, he could travel with ease in any social circle. She would also be an asset to his business.

Yes, she would suit his needs nicely, in bed and out. After he seduced her, and he would, maybe he could con himself into believing she could make him clean on the inside, too.

* * *

The helicopter hovered over eastern Pennsylvania, landing on a helipad next to the lake, and what looked like a compound. A man approached the helicopter and took the luggage. Leo jumped out and helped Calista onto the ground, moving swiftly toward a vehicle waiting on the drive.

Moments later, they pulled into the back driveway of a three-story luxury mansion that sat directly on the lake. "Good for a little break, don't you think?" he asked as he led her into the huge house.

"Or longer," she said, taking in the polished wood floors and beautiful furnishings. More evidence that the con man had done very well for himself. He guided her to the room facing the lake and she stared out at the beautiful blue water and could have almost happily died from the serene view of the sunset.

"This is so beautiful. How do you tear yourself away?" she asked. "The view is just—" She broke off without adequate words to describe it.

"I get restless if I'm in one place too long," he said. "Plus, business can be very demanding."

"Hmm," she said and met his gaze. "If you say so."

He chuckled. "I bet you don't stay still for long either," he said.

She didn't, for other reasons, though. "Maybe, but this could tempt me."

"Good," he said, gazing at her through hooded eyes. "Dinner will be waiting for us on the terrace. Steak and lobster." A woman approached them. "Denise will show you to your room while I make some calls."

Denise led her to a beautiful room furnished with a queen-size bed, furniture upholstered in a soft pastel palette and Monet prints. The result was so soothing Calista could have happily closed the door and lived there the rest of her existence if she didn't have other responsibilities. She sank into a chair next to the window. Drinking in the peaceful reflection the moon cast on the lake, she felt her tension fade away. For a few sweet seconds, she felt safe.

A knock sounded on her door and the feeling disappeared. She must not forget that she was here for a reason. Calista stood and answered the door. "Yes?" she said to Denise.

"Mr. Grant invites you to join him for dinner," the woman said.

"Thank you," Calista said and grabbed her sweater. Peace was an illusion. She needed to continue with her strategy. "I'm ready now."

Denise led her to a porch that featured an outdoor heater. It was a clear night and she felt surrounded by the stars. "It's beautiful," she murmured.

"Yes it is," Denise said. "Mr. Grant will be here momentarily."

Sitting down next to the heater, she listened to the lap of the water against the shore. It didn't get any better than this.

Leo appeared and she met his gaze. "This is heaven. I don't care what your work demands are. I still can't comprehend how you can leave this place."

"You like it?" he said with an approving smile.

"What's not to like? Beautiful scenery, comfortable living conditions." She sighed.

"I'm glad you like it," he said.

"And have you noticed the stars?" she asked, looking up at the sky.

"No, but I would expect you to," he said. "See anything interesting up there?"

"It's more than interesting," she whispered.

"I may have to get a telescope so you can show me how interesting it is," he said.

A staff member appeared with a tray of food and served both of them. "It looks delicious," she said.

"No more than you," he said.

She bit her lip and looked down at her food. "What made you decide to build a lake home here if you fight staying here?"

"Something about it was irresistible," he said. "I missed the water. I miss the ocean too," he said. "I'll address the ocean another time."

"How can you miss the water? Haven't you spent your whole life in Philly?"

He paused. "No. I have vague memories of visiting the sea. I can't explain it. I just do."

She frowned, taking a bite of lobster. "But you said you had no childhood."

"Exactly," he said in a crisp voice. "Like I said, I can't explain it. It's like it's from another life. One of the few irrational things about me." He took a bite of steak.

She sensed he didn't want to discuss it further. Despite her desire to ask more, she delayed giving in to her curiosity. She had another job to do. "Thank you for inviting me. After the prom drama of the day, this is a huge relief."

He smiled. "How did that go?"

"Mostly good," she said. "My sisters are total opposites. Tami can be a trial, but she was good today."

"How often do you see them?" he asked.

"Almost every week," she said. "The love of my life."

He slid his hand across the table and covered hers. "Is that why you're not married?" he asked.

"It's more complicated than that. I guess I haven't found the right man yet," she said.

"Describe the right man," he said. "Similar backgrounds? Shared passage on the Mayflower? Same schools?"

"No," she said, laughing at the Mayflower comment. "Good head, good heart and crazy for me."

"That list doesn't sound that difficult," he said.

"You'd be surprised," she said. "What about you? Describe your right woman."

"Someone classier than I am to conceal my rough edges," he said. "Beauty doesn't hurt. Complete honesty. I'm not sure marriage is necessary, though."

"Many men don't," she said in a dry tone, her stomach tightening at his reference to honesty. How could he expect that of someone when he'd been the consummate liar?

"You disagree?"

"I believe in family. Marriage is part of family."

He shrugged. "I don't know much about family."

She gave a shrug in return. "Maybe you should learn."

He paused as he lifted his beer. "Is that a challenge?"

"I'll let you decide that," she said with a light laugh.

After dinner, they took a walk along the long dock that led out to the lake. His cell phone beeped and he glanced at the caller ID. "Excuse me, I need to take this. Won't be a minute. I've had a few blips with the China deal." He put the phone to his ear. "Leo Grant," he said and listened.

Calista walked further down the dock, torn between her next step with Leo and the sound of his voice.

"So our shipping agent in Hong Kong tried to charge more after we'd already loaded the merchandise for transport? Fine. Pay the surcharge this once, then call our second choice. After delivery is confirmed, cut the first guy loose and tell him we will be reporting his behavior to everyone in the shipping and merchandising business."

The ruthless tone in his voice made her throat tighten.

"That's my final word," he said. He turned off his cell and looked toward her. "That's done. We shouldn't have any more interruptions this evening," he said and moved beside her, sliding his arm behind her back.

"Why do I get the feeling that a guillotine has just fallen on some very foolish guy in Hong Kong?" she asked.

Leo shrugged. "He should have stuck to the deal. If someone tries to cheat me, they're history."

She felt a chill and a sliver of bitterness at his hypocrisy. How many times had his own father cheated people? How many times had Leo been a part of his father's schemes?

"Have I frightened you?" he asked. "There's no need as long as you're honest with me," he said, drawing her against him as he leaned against the small building at the far end of the pier. "Now let me make you forget about that unpleasant phone call."

His warmth surrounded her as he slid his hands down her back to her bottom and slid one of his hard thighs between her legs. A stab of sensual shock raced through her. "Leo," she began.

He dipped his head to her throat, rubbing his lips over her skin. "I bet every inch of you tastes delicious," he muttered, sliding his tongue over a sensitive spot. "I knew you would from the first minute I met you. Give me your mouth," he said and coaxed her lips into meeting his. Skimming one of his hands upward, he touched the side of her breast.

He emanated pure masculine strength and sexuality

and gave her the unmistakable message that he wanted to possess her. The primitive drive seemed to throb just beneath his clothes. Despite every reason she had to detest him, she was drawn to him like no other man. Here, she sensed, was a man with a will to match her own. Without conscious thought, she responded to him, sliding her arms up behind his neck, arching against him.

He took her mouth and she took his, drawing his tongue into the recesses. Heat scored her from the inside out, and her body called to his. His touch was tender, edged with roughness that only turned her on more.

He gave a low, carnal growl. "Let's go back to the house. I want you in my bed."

His words threw her into a maelstrom of confusion. She drew back from him catching her breath, trying to catch her sanity. She wanted to be with him intimately. She wanted him. But she had a plan. This relationship wasn't for her pleasure. It was for something far more important.

She inhaled another deep breath, reaching down deep for her conviction. "I want—" She broke off when she looked into his dark needy gaze and her mouth went dry. She couldn't look into his eyes at this close range. His gaze reflected the ache she felt inside her. She bit her lip and closed her eyes. "I'm afraid you're not going to understand this."

"Understand what?" he asked.

She forced her eyes open, but turned her gaze to his right shoulder. His strong, broad shoulder. "I want to go to bed with you."

"Good, let's—"

"But I can't," she quickly added.

Silence, so clear she could hear the water lapping against the dock, followed.

"Why?" he asked.

Summoning her courage, she met his gaze. "It's going to sound terribly old-fashioned, but I want to keep that for the man I marry. I don't think I'm cut out to be intimate with a lot of men. I don't want to make the mistake of giving my heart, myself, to a man and then being crushed because he isn't the right one."

He shot her a considering look then wiped his hand over his face. "You're telling me that you're saving yourself for marriage? That's the oldest trick in the book."

"I told you that you wouldn't understand. I'll leave in the morning," she said and turned away from him to walk back to the house. She crossed her arms over her chest, feeling the impending crush of defeat. Holding off on sex had been a calculated risk, but Calista had suspected that it would be difficult to motivate Leo to marry her quickly unless she waited.

Three seconds later, she felt her hand caught by his. "Not so fast," he said.

She stopped in surprise, searching his face.

"The least you can do is give me a chance to change your mind. Or see if you can change mine," he said.

Her heart racing a mile a minute, she shook her head. "I don't want to deceive you. I heard you talking earlier. You hate to be tricked. Again, it's best if I leave in the morning."

He lifted her hand to his mouth. "I'm not disappointed, or feeling tricked. I'm just surprised. Your outlook is unusual."

"I know, but I've watched so many of my friends make poor choices and wish they could take everything back. It's about more than the physical intimacy. I just think I'm one of those women who jumps all the way into the pool of commitment. I totally understand if you're not looking for that. Most men aren't." She added that last statement to spur his competitive nature. Leo wouldn't want to be compared to another man.

"I'm not most men," he said. "I'll show you to your guest room and we'll see how it goes."

She opened her mouth to tell him she had judged him correctly, but he covered her mouth with his finger. "I insist," he said in the sexiest voice she'd ever heard.

After Leo led Calista to the guest bedroom, he prowled his balcony, still aroused from the way she'd tasted, smelled and felt in his arms. He couldn't remember a time when a woman had turned him away from her bed. Although she'd done it without malice, it didn't diminish his sexual frustration. In fact, her desire not to manipulate him aroused him even more.

Many women had tried to trick him into marriage. A few had even feigned signs of pregnancy, but Leo had been very careful. He had no interest in binding himself to just any woman. At least, he hadn't until now. But he saw the advantage of linking himself with Calista. She was pure. She represented a fresh start.

Glancing out at the still lake, he considered taking a dip in the frigid water to quiet the heat Calista had generated in him and the longings he'd buried long ago. Did he really want a family? Was such a thing possible for him? His upbringing had been one move after another. He'd never known when his guardian father would take out his rage on him. He'd spent so many years braced for something horrible to happen to him. And it had, several times until he'd run away.

Leo wondered what it would be like to be loved by a

woman like Calista. He sensed she was the kind of woman who would marry forever. Look at her commitment to her sisters. She possessed a strength that drew him like a light in the darkness.

Was he considering marrying her? The notion shocked him. He barely knew her. Yet, he knew she was different. She'd known what it was like to be raised in a loving family—with relationships and ties she still worked to keep strong. She possessed the core of something he'd been searching for, for years.

He raked his hand through his hair. It wasn't just sex. He suspected he could seduce her into his bed despite her lofty goal. The sexual animal in him roared at the urge to take her, to make her his. He could and he suspected they would bring each other amazing pleasure.

For some strange, insane reason, however, he hesitated seducing her for the pure purpose of his gratification. It wasn't out of consideration for her principles. No. Her reticence called to his competitive nature. He wanted her to be convinced that he was the man she wanted. The man she couldn't turn down. He wanted her to come to him.

The next morning after breakfast, Leo took Calista out on his boat.

"The water is beautiful," she told him when they stopped near another pier.

"Want to swim?" he asked.

"I don't know," she said, giving the lake a skeptical glance. "How cold is it?"

"Depends on whether you're cold-blooded or warm-blooded," he said and stripped off his shirt. "Let's go in."

He felt her gaze linger on his chest then she seemed to

force her gaze away from him. "If you're sure," she said. "If I freeze, you have to promise to pull me out. Okay?"

"Promise," he said and watched her remove her shirt to reveal a bikini top that encased her full, creamy breasts. He could easily imagine them bare and wondered about the color and size of her nipples.

She kicked off her shoes to reveal slender feet with vixen-red toenails. He liked that touch of wildness she kept hidden from the rest of the world. He'd like to take care of all her wild urges. She pushed down her jeans, wiggling as she stepped out of them.

He fixated on the inviting curves of her waist and hips, feeling himself respond to the sight of her feminine figure. He took action to cool his arousal immediately. Diving into the water, he felt the cold wetness sink into his skin. Rising to the surface, he caught sight of her looking down at him from the boat.

"How cold is it?"

"Not cold enough to make icebergs," he said.

"That's not very encouraging," she said.

"Are you afraid?" he asked.

She immediately pursed her lips and lifted her chin. "Absolutely not," she said and jumped off the side of the boat. Seconds later, she bobbed to the ladder, gasping. "Omigod, you lied. This water is frigid."

"Well, it's not as warm as my pool at the house," he said, swimming toward her. "But it could be worse."

"When?" she asked. "In January?"

He laughed.

A wake from a boat riding past caused a wave and she reached for him with fear in her eyes. Concern rushed through him. "You're okay," he said, pulling her body against his. "I wouldn't let you drown. Damn, I should have asked if you're a swimmer."

"Of course I am," she said, her wide green eyes meeting his. Another wave rolled toward them and she clung to him more tightly.

"Are you afraid?" he asked, enjoying the sensation of her lithe body against his.

"Not really," she said, but her tone wasn't at all convincing.

"Nice try. You can tell me the truth now," he said, lifting her chin to meet his gaze again.

She shook her head and sighed. "It's silly."

"I bet not," he said.

"One time when I was a teenager, a friend invited me to the lake. Her father took us out in his boat. I didn't know it, but he'd had too much to drink. It was a windy, choppy day. I fell overboard and hit my head against the side of the boat."

Leo swore. "Why didn't you tell me? I wouldn't have forced you into the water."

"You didn't force me. Besides, I don't like it that I still get that knot in my stomach when I think about lakes and boats. Being a wuss is such a bore."

He admired her for trying to rise above her fear. "You could never be a bore."

"Just trying to be a brave little toaster," she said with a smile.

Her vulnerability grabbed at him, making him feel incredibly protective. "We can go back."

"No," she protested. "It's so beautiful here. I just might not be able to stand the water temperature very long. Although you are helping," she said, her eyelashes sweeping downward, shielding her eyes from him.

Despite the chilly water, arousal shot through him again. "Good to know I'm useful in some way," he said, sliding his hands around her back. The sunlight glistened on her light blond hair and the water droplets on her fair skin. He fought a strong urge to lick those droplets.

Instead, he took her mouth in a kiss. Her lips reminded him of the finest brandy, potent and addicting. He drew her tongue into his mouth and she made a delicious sound of arousal. Leo wanted to hear that sound again and again. He felt her shiver, but he wasn't sure if it was from arousal or cold.

"Let's go back to the house," he said and pulled her toward the ladder to the boat. "But you should know that when we ride on the boat the breeze will make you even colder."

"We could fish," she said.

He blinked, surprised at her suggestion. "You know how?"

"Of course," she said. "Do you? If you don't, I can show you."

He laughed at the lightning-fast switch from uncertainty to confidence. "I can fish," he said. "A long time ago, I fished for my supper."

She met his gaze. "Was that before or after you were hatched at the age of sixteen?"

"Both," he said and turned her toward the ladder. "You go first and I'll bring up the rear." She climbed the rungs and he was given an up close view of her gorgeous derriere in her bikini bottom. He groaned, wondering if he would be able to stick to his plan to make her come to him.

* * *

Hours later, Leo watched her lean back in the Jacuzzi and sigh. "What a great day," she said, then cracked open one eyelid. "Too bad the fish I caught was so much bigger than yours."

He chuckled. "Lady's luck," he said. "I couldn't show you up. You're my guest."

She opened both her eyes and scowled. "That's pure bull. The next thing you'll be doing is telling me you're not competitive."

"Only every bone in my body," he said.

She smiled and her gaze dipped to his shoulders in feminine appreciation. She'd done that several times today, so he knew she wasn't immune to him. He was winning her inch by inch. The notion filled him with a rush he hadn't experienced in a long time.

"Like the hot tub?" he asked.

She nodded, closing her eyes again.

"It's even better when you're naked," he said.

She opened her eyes to sexy slits. "And how would you know that?"

"It's in the manufacturer's instructions," he said.

A gusty laugh from her rippled all the way down his body to his groin.

"I dare you to take off your swimsuit," he said.

"I'm not sure that's a good idea," she said with a sigh.

"Even if I promise to keep my hands off of you?" he asked.

"The problem," she said as she moved closer to him and he pulled her onto his lap, "is that I won't want your to keep you hands off of me."

Three

As the helicopter landed on top of the high-rise in Philadelphia, Leo took Calista's hand and helped her onto the ground. Within moments, George was driving them in a limo toward her apartment. She turned to Leo. "This has been an incredible twenty-four hours. Thank you for everything."

"I'm glad you enjoyed yourself," he said and lifted his finger to stroke her cheek. "It doesn't have to end."

His touch distracted her, making her heart beat erratically. "What do you mean?"

"I'd like you to move in with me," he said.

Calista blinked, surprised by his speed and decisiveness. "Wow," she said. "That's fast." She took a breath. "It's very tempting, but as I've told you, I really want to be married before I live with a man."

"Why is that so important to you?" he asked with more than a trace of irritation on his face.

"I told you that I believe in family. A husband, wife and children can provide the ultimate joy, security and comfort for each other. I want that for myself. I want to give it to someone else," she said, her gut twisting because although she believed what she was saying, she knew it wouldn't come true for her.

"Was your upbringing that idyllic?"

She looked away, feeling a stab of shame about her father's financial disaster and death that never seemed to go away. "Of course not," she said. "Maybe because it wasn't idyllic, I'm determined to have something different for myself. It may sound crazy to you, but I want the security of family and a strong man."

He paused a moment, his dark gaze full of conflicting feelings. "It doesn't sound crazy. I just don't have much experience in that area." He covered her hand with his. "I want to spend more time with you."

"I want the same," she said quietly.

"Then come and live with me in my apartment. I'll make sure you won't regret it," he said, lifting her hand to his lips.

Even though they hadn't known each other long, Calista was more than a little tempted. There was a strength about Leo that drew something from deep inside her. His magnetism almost made her forget her purpose with him. Almost. His charm, though, belied any chance for security. He was accustomed to getting what he wanted from women without making a commitment. She wondered if she would possibly be able to seduce him to the point of marriage. Doubt surged through her.

"I'm sorry. I can't. I just can't," she said and fought the

fear that rose in her throat. "I really do understand if you don't want to continue with me. I'm sure you're used to a different kind of arrangement with women." She glanced outside the window. "Maybe we shouldn't have gone out in the first place, but I just couldn't resist you."

The limo stopped in front of her apartment building. She turned to Leo. "Thank you again for a wonderful time."

He helped her out of the limo and walked her to the security entrance. "My pleasure," he said. "Good night, Calista."

Calista tried to read his inscrutable expression and felt a sinking sensation in the pit of her stomach. He'd decided she wasn't worth the wait or the effort. She watched him walk out of her lobby and most likely out of her life. Though her ego stung, she was far more worried about her sisters' futures.

Swearing under her breath, she took the elevator to her small apartment. What was she going to do now? Pacing the length of her den, she tried to summon a plan B. If she went to bed with Leo, she would have no hope of marrying him. Plus, even though she found him physically attractive, she wasn't sure when her real feelings and thoughts about what he'd done to her father would leak past her facade. What if she slipped and told him she felt he was responsible? If he knew the truth…

Calista squeezed her eyes shut, feeling hopeless and trapped. She hated being deceptive, but she'd made this decision and she wasn't going to castigate herself for it. Her sisters deserved a good education and a better start than they'd had. They'd suffered the brunt of her family's implosion because of their youth. She would never be able to erase the shattered expressions on her sisters' faces when first her father had died and then less than two years later, they'd lost Mom, too.

Her head throbbing with tension, Calista tried to calm herself. Maybe she'd misread Leo. Maybe he would call her again.

Two weeks later, after no word from Leo, Calista saw the writing on the wall. Leo wasn't going to call. He was done with her. Bummed, but still obligated to attend the Brother-Sister Charity Auction, she accepted an invitation from Robert Powell, a man who worked in her office building. Amusing and seemingly easygoing, he'd asked her out several times. She hoped Robert could distract her from her disappointment.

Wearing a Betsey Johnson Spring dress she'd bought on sale, she greeted Robert in her lobby. His appreciative look provided a balm to her still smarting ego. At the auction, Calista mingled and introduced Robert to her acquaintances.

He slid his arm around her waist. "Do you realize I've been asking you out for months? You're worth the wait," he said and dipped his gaze suggestively over her.

Not wanting to encourage the flicker of sensual interest she glimpsed in his gaze, she shook her head. "Oh, not really. I'm not worth the wait at all. I'm just the good friend type, you know. Boring, works too much. All that."

He gave a low chuckle. "I don't think so."

"Calista." A voice that had haunted her captured her attention. "How are you?"

She swung around to see Leo Grant, larger than life, staring down at her. She might have needed to pinch herself if not for the gorgeous brunette on his arm. She forced her lips into a smile, thinking he hadn't waited long to replace her. "Fine, thank you."

"And your friend," Leo said, his gaze assessing Robert. "We haven't met."

"Robert Powell, this is Leo Grant," she said, refusing to inquire about *his* escort. The men exchanged handshakes. "Oh, look, they're starting the auction. I'm helping behind the scenes. I'll see you afterward, Robert. Please excuse me," she said and turned away.

Upset, she balled her fists at her side and strode toward the side of the ballroom where the items for auction were displayed. Forcing any thought of Leo from her head, she focused on tagging the items with the winners' names. After about forty-five minutes, the volunteer coordinator sent her for a break and she got a glass of water from the bar.

On her way back, Leo stepped in front of her, his eyes dark with what looked like anger. "You didn't waste any time, did you?" he asked.

"I could say the same for you," she retorted.

"She's the daughter of a friend I owed a favor," he said. "Not that I should have to explain myself."

"How convenient that she's drop-dead gorgeous. It must be a total chore to escort her."

He tilted his head and narrowed his eyes. "I could almost believe you're jealous."

"You would be wrong," she told him and moved to step around him.

He stopped her, his hand closing around her wrist like a handcuff. "Let's take this discussion somewhere private," he said and led her away from the crowd. He opened the door to an empty room, pulled her inside and closed the door behind him.

"Who is this Robert? Is he important to you?" he demanded.

Nervous, yet strangely thrilled to see him, she lifted her chin. "What's it to you? You haven't called me for two weeks."

"I've been out of the country."

She gave an indignant shrug. "I'm sure your cell phone has reception from everywhere in the world and maybe a few planets, too."

"Okay," he said. "I didn't want to call you. I wanted to give myself some time away from you. I didn't want to do anything impulsive."

Her heart hammered in her chest.

"You still haven't answered my question about Robert. Do you have feelings for him?" he asked flatly.

"No," she said. "No more than I would a friend. He's asked me out for months and I've turned him down."

"Then why did you agree to go out with him tonight?"

She paused and looked away with a sigh. "I was moping," she confessed.

"Excuse me?" he said.

She glanced back at him, peeved. "You heard me. I said I was moping. Because you haven't called me," she added reluctantly.

His eyes glittered as he looked at her. "Okay, I've thought about it for the last two weeks and made a decision. We'll get married."

Calista dropped her jaw in shock. "Excuse me?"

"I said we'll get married. I'd prefer just a living arrangement because of the legalities, but we can take care of that with a prenup." He paused, studying her carefully. "Unless you're adverse to a prenup."

Her thoughts still spinning as she tried to take it all in, she shook her head. "No, but—"

"Were you planning on a large formal ceremony? I understand women spend their entire lives mentally planning their dream weddings," he said as if the thought of it seemed insane to him.

"I suppose some do. I'd always thought I would want something small," she said. Calista had left fairy-tale wedding land shortly after her father's death. Her primary focus had been on survival, not having a huge society wedding.

"Good," he said in approval. "Then it's settled. I can have one of my assistants get together with you to make the arrangements. She knows the dates I'm available."

She held up her hand. "Wait just a second. You're moving at warp speed and I'm still trying to catch up. What made you think to get married?"

"I tried to put you out of my mind during the last two weeks. I found I didn't want to," he said.

Given the fact that they hadn't known each other very long, she was surprised at how his words got under her skin. It was a far cry from hearts and flowers. "I don't know what to say."

"Yes," he said.

She bit her lip and couldn't swallow a chuckle. "You didn't ask."

"Will you marry me?" he asked without missing a beat, his dark gaze holding hers.

"This is crazy," she whispered. Her heart lurched. After all her planning, could she really do this?

"Is that your answer?" he asked.

"No," she said, her lungs squeezing so tight she couldn't breathe. It was the best solution for Tina and Tami. His father owed her family for what he had taken from them. It was necessary. "Yes, yes."

Leo sat on the deck of his lakefront home the night before his wedding and shared Scotch with George. Calista and her family would arrive tomorrow morning via his helicopter. All the arrangements had been made. The only thing Leo had to do was show up at the ceremony tomorrow at noon and make sure not to see Calista before then. She had insisted. Silly superstition, but he would play along for her ease. With each passing day, she had seemed to grow more nervous.

George lifted his shot glass in salute. "I never thought I would see the day when you would marry a woman only a month after meeting her. Good luck to ya."

Leo shot George a sideways glance and lifted his glass. "Thank you. You haven't said much about my bride-to-be."

"What's to say?" George asked. "She's beautiful." He shrugged and tossed back the scotch, setting his glass down for a refill. "There's just something about her."

"What?" Leo asked, his antennae on alert. George was an excellent judge of character.

George frowned and squinted his eyes. "I can't put my finger on it. She's not evil," he said. "But there's something going on beneath the surface. The woman's more complicated than she seems."

Leo twirled the thought around in his head. "Most intelligent women are complicated."

"True," George said, nodding his head. "How'd the prenup go?"

"I insisted she have her attorney look at it. He put in a clause about her getting ten million after six months," Leo said. "Mine cut it down to two million. Her attorney didn't like it, but she signed." He shrugged. "She's so family-focused that I'm sure this wasn't her idea. It had to have come from her attorney."

"You're sure she doesn't know your guardian helped bring down her father?" George asked.

"How could she?" Leo asked, the familiar taste of bitterness filling his mouth at the mention of Clyde Hawkins. "It was ten years ago, and I've wiped out my association with him. Besides, that was one scheme I didn't play. I may have been introduced as Clyde's genius, gifted son, but I didn't have to do anything but validate Clyde's super success."

"Why are you marrying her?" George asked bluntly.

Not many would have the nerve to question his decisions, but he trusted George more than he trusted anyone else. "Besides the fact that I want to have sex with her?"

George chuckled. "Yes."

"I want the expanding Japanese and Indian markets, and I'm finding that the leaders of the companies I'm negotiating with aren't comfortable with my single status. I'm competing with other companies for the business. It's time to get a wife. Calista fits the bill. She's well educated and beautiful. She'll be an asset."

"So this is a business decision?" George asked.

"Mostly," Leo said. "The timing is good—no long engagement period."

George clicked his shot glass against his again. "I wish you a happy home then, Leo. After all you've been through, you deserve something good. I hope Calista will be good for you."

* * *

Calista practiced yoga breathing as the helicopter descended to Leo's helipad at the lake. In a matter of hours, she would be married.

"Omigod, this is amazing," Tami said, lifting her cell phone toward the window and taking a picture. "I have to text my boyfriend a photo. Will there be a photographer at the ceremony?"

"Yes," Calista said, taking another deep breath.

"Are you okay?" Tina asked. "You look whiter than usual."

"It's the helicopter," Calista insisted and forced a smile. "Did you enjoy the ride?"

"It was *sweet*," Tina said.

"What about you, Justin?" she asked her nephew.

"Cool," he said, clearly trying to appear unimpressed but not quite succeeding. "I want one of these when I grow up."

Sharon laughed. "Keep your grades up and go to college and you may have a shot at it."

The helicopter landed and several members of Leo's staff stood to greet them. A man helped her sisters, cousin, her cousin's husband and son out of the helicopter. Calista found herself pausing before she accepted the assistance of a man to help her step onto the ground. Every passing second drew her closer to the time when she would become Leo Grant's wife. Her heart raced in fear at the thought, then she looked at her sisters. So young, yet their childhoods had been stolen from them. The least she could do was to give them some security now and a solid start for their adult lives.

"Miss French," the man said, having been schooled in her appearance. She wondered from where Leo or his assistant had pulled her photograph, then pushed the thought aside.

"Thank you very much," she said and smiled.

"My name is Henry. I'm in charge of Mr. Grant's lake home. I have a special suite for you to dress for the ceremony. Mr. Grant has ordered rooms and food for the rest of your family," he said, guiding her down the walk. "I'm told that the second you are sequestered in your suite, I am to call Mr. Grant. He is in a room facing away from the lake."

She smiled. So, he had stuck to the agreement not to see her before the wedding. She had to like him for that. Her stomach dipped again. She would need to exhibit far more than like in their wedding bed tonight. She was terrified her true feelings for Leo would show.

Following Henry toward the suite, she heard her sisters gasp in approval as they walked inside Leo's home. *"Sweet,"* Tami said. "More pics."

"I can't remember being in a house this beautiful," Tina said, looking around.

Calista felt a twist of regret that she hadn't been able to provide more for her young sisters after her parents' deaths.

Her cousin studied her and broke away from her husband to come to Calista's side. "You need someone to help you get ready," Sharon insisted.

"I'll be fine. Just a little repair work on my hair and face, pull up my dress and I'm done," Calista said, the strange sensation of panic and numbness filling her again.

Sharon frowned. "I'll hang around anyway. A bride shouldn't be alone on her wedding day."

Perhaps her cousin was right. Calista was feeling the

unmistakable surge of fight-or-flight syndrome, and at the moment flight seemed most possible.

"This way, ladies," Henry said, guiding them up a curved stairway. "Jamal will take the rest of you to your rooms. Refreshments will be waiting."

"Thank goodness, I'm starving," Justin muttered.

"See you soon, bridie," Tami said with a broad smile.

"See you soon," Calista replied with much less enthusiasm.

Sharon helped Calista get dressed and encouraged her to eat. Calista couldn't swallow a bite. Even though this was the best possible result from her plan, she couldn't believe it was happening so fast.

"You look dazed and pale, sweetheart. Are you okay?" Sharon asked, her face full of worry.

"Just wedding-day jitters," Calista said with a smile.

"Are you sure this is what you want?" Sharon asked. "You haven't known Leo very long at all."

Calista recited her rehearsed response, "When it's right, it's right."

"But still," Sharon said, frowning.

A knock sounded on the door. "Oh, could you please get that?" she asked, thankful for the interruption. The photographer appeared. "Ready for me to take a few shots?"

"Of course," she said, smoothing her dress with her hands. "Sharon, come stand here with me."

Sharon shook her head shyly. "Oh, no. It's your time to shine. You look beautiful."

"But I want my close family members with me," Calista said. "Please get my sisters and bring them here."

Calista posed for several pictures before her sisters and Sharon returned. Then she took several pictures with them. Tami took a few pics with her cell phone. Calista drank in the sight of her happy sisters and reminded herself repeatedly that they were the reason she was doing this. Their lives would be so much better because she was marrying Leo.

One of Leo's staff poked her head in the doorway. "It's time," she said with a smile. "Are you ready?"

"Yes," Tami and Tina chorused, giggling with excitement.

Sharon placed a kiss on Calista's cheek. "I'll see you on the dock. You can still change your mind," she said.

How I wish. Calista smiled instead. "I'm all decided. Thank you for coming today."

"Wouldn't miss it," Sharon said. "Be happy."

Happiness for herself was the last thing on Calista's mind as she and her sisters walked down the staircase. Just before they stepped outside, Tami turned to her and adjusted her veil. "You really do look beautiful. Leo is one lucky dude."

Calista laughed. "You're sweet. Both of you look gorgeous yourselves."

"Do we really get to go for a boat ride after the ceremony?" Tina asked.

"Sure do. We're changing clothes and eating on Leo's yacht," Calista said. "Now let's get this over—" She barely caught herself. "Let's get this wedding on its way."

On either side of her, her sisters escorted her down to the dock. As she rounded the corner, she saw the minister, George and Leo. Her heart felt as if it dipped to her feet at the sight of him. Dressed in a designer black suit with a crisp white shirt and crimson tie, she knew the second he saw her. She felt the weight and heat of his gaze from yards away.

"Ready?" Tami asked. "Why did you stop?"

Calista had been so distracted she hadn't even noticed she wasn't moving forward. Tami glanced in the direction of Calista's gaze and gave a sigh. "He's pretty hot, isn't he?"

"Tami," Tina whispered. "Show some dignity. This is a wedding."

"You were the one ready to go jump on a boat before we'd even gotten to the dock," Tami retorted.

"Girls, you're supposed to be escorting me. Please stop arguing," Calista said, gritting her teeth. She began to walk again.

She felt Leo's gaze take her in from head to toe and wondered if he approved of the full-length A-line ivory chiffon gown with fitted sweetheart bodice that suddenly felt as if it was suffocating her. Her hair was half up, half down in loose curls. Pearl drop earrings dangled from her ears. She felt like a sacrificial bride from the Regency period.

Mentally rolling her eyes at herself, she stiffened her spine. *Cut the martyr act.* She was a woman taking control of her and her sisters' destinies. She only had to last six months. Not a lifetime.

She finally stood opposite the minister and focused her attention on the kindly faced man for a moment while she wondered if she would burn in hell for what she was doing. She felt a stab of guilt and brushed it aside. She couldn't have done this to just anyone. She'd chosen Leo because of what his father had done to her family. In the scheme of things, it was fair. It wasn't as if he would miss the money.

Lord, what thoughts to have while she was getting married. "Who gives this bride?" the minister asked.

"We do," Tami and Tina said and giggled. Tami took Calista's hand and reached for Leo's, then put them together. "Be good to my sister," she whispered to Leo. "Or I'll make your life a living hell. Ask Aunt Sharon. I can do it."

Leo blinked and shot Calista a bemused look. Embarrassed, Calista shook her head and mouthed *teenagers*. Leo's mouth lifted in a half grin and he nodded, both his hands enclosing hers.

Within seconds, she was held captive by his gaze as he began to recite the vows. "I, Leonardo Grant, take you Calista French…"

The rest of the ceremony passed in a daze. She looked down at the diamond and platinum band Leo placed on her finger. Was this real? Was this happening?

"Calista," Leo whispered. "Ring."

Biting her lip, she took the platinum band from Tina and pushed it down his finger. His hands were so much larger than hers, warmer and stronger. In a different lifetime, she wondered if she could have trusted him, relied on him. She remembered what his father had done and dismissed the thought. Deep, underneath it all, Leo was a liar, and she'd just joined with him in the biggest lie of her life.

"I now pronounce you husband and wife. You may kiss your bride."

Leo lowered his head and took her mouth with a kiss of possession and the promise of passion. He'd done his part. Now she would have to do hers.

Less than an hour later, they changed clothes and took Leo's yacht for a ride around the lake. After a late lunch that she didn't consume because she was still too nervous to eat, her sisters and Justin went for a swim. Leo made friendly small talk with all of her family. He promised her sisters that he would take them skiing next time they visited.

All too soon, the sun faded and the air turned chilly. The yacht returned to the dock and Calista kissed her family goodbye before Leo's helicopter took them away. She watched them go, fighting a feeling of abandonment. She felt Leo slide his hand behind her back and around her waist and closed her eyes, girding herself for the night to come.

"Thank you for letting them come," she said. "It meant a lot to me."

"You're welcome," he said, his lips twitching. "As long as Tami doesn't come after me with any sharp objects."

She laughed despite the way her stomach twisted with nerves. "She's a big bluffer. Very dramatic and emotional. She's the one who has asthma. She gives Sharon and me hives with some of the things she does, but she's got a big heart."

"Like her sister," he said and began to lead her back to the house.

"Hmm," she said in a noncommittal voice.

"You haven't eaten anything all day," he said.

She glanced up at him again, taking in his hard jaw and the sheer maleness of his physique. "How do you know?"

"My staff told me you ate nothing before the wedding, and I noticed that you ate nothing on the boat. Except for one bite of the cake."

"It was a big day."

"Yes, so I want you to eat something now. What shall I ask my staff to bring you?"

"I hate to bother them."

"You're not bothering," he said impatiently. "They are paid to do this. They spend a lot of time bored, so they're actually glad to have something to do."

Skeptical, she shot him a sideways glance. "Who told you that? Someone who wanted a raise?"

He chuckled. "If you don't tell me what you want, then I'll order a five-course meal."

"A turkey sandwich," she said quickly.

"Done," he said and squeezed her shoulders. She was still surprised at how kind he'd been to her sisters. She hadn't expected him to be an ogre, just distantly polite. Instead, he'd been charming. With his arm around her, she could almost believe he felt protective of her. Almost.

Four

Leo drank a beer while he watched Calista take a few bites of her turkey sandwich. Her gaze skittered from his and she took tiny sips from her water. It took him a moment to read her, but then realization jolted him. She was *nervous*. He'd noticed her nerves at the wedding, but assumed they would pass after the vow-taking.

She was still on edge, he noticed, and felt a foreign twist of tenderness toward her. Virginal nerves, he concluded. In this day and age, who would have thought it? There was no need to worry, he thought as he took in the sight of her. He could have easily seduced her before now. Some odd sense of ethics he hadn't known he possessed had made him pause.

No need for that anymore, he realized as he watched her lick her lips after she took another drink of water. "The sandwich was a good idea, thanks," she said.

"I frequently have good ideas," he said, holding her gaze.

"I'm sure you do," she said.

"It's been a long day," he said. "We should go upstairs."

Calista's heart jumped into her throat. She'd known this would happen. Leo was now her husband. He would pay for the security of her sisters' future and she would pay by being his wife, albeit temporarily. Part of her couldn't dismiss the fact that this man was connected to her father's financial failure and subsequent death. In a way it would be making love with the devil.

She took a deep breath. There was no need to be melodramatic now. Leo was just a man, not a god or a devil. Right? Why was she so apprehensive? It wasn't as if she…

Stiffening her spine, she told herself to buck up to her end of the deal. "Can I grab another water?" she asked with a smile.

"I have plenty in my room." He extended his hand and his gaze fell over her like the heat from a midafternoon scorching summer day. She took his hand and he led her upstairs, stopping at his bedroom door to open it. Before she realized it, he swooped her up into his arms and carried her inside.

"Oh," she said. "A surprise."

"It's a tradition. Since you're a new bride, I thought you might enjoy it," he said, his face close to hers.

All too aware of his strength, she spotted a bottle of champagne and a tray of strawberries next to the huge bed that seemed to dominate the wall facing the windows. Lit candles provided a seductive ambiance. She clung to his shoulders. "I didn't know you were much for traditions."

"I'm not," he said. "But I don't have to buck all of them."

He set her down on the bed. "Now we can have a private toast," he said and popped open the champagne. He spilled the light golden liquid into one flute then another.

Giving her one of the glasses, he lifted his own. "To us and all the traditions we'll make and break together." He clicked his glass against hers. "Starting tonight."

Her heart hammered at the expression on his face. He looked as if he could literally consume her. She'd known he was highly sexual from the first time she'd seen him in person, but now she wondered if she would be able to... Pushing the thought from her mind again, she nodded and took a long drink of champagne, then another. She suspected, however, that she would need to consume the entire bottle to bring her anxiousness under control.

Leo sat on the bed and lifted his hand to cup her cheek. "There's no need to be nervous."

"I'm not," she said. "Really."

His lips lifted in a half grin. "You just need something else to think about," he said and lowered his mouth to hers. His lips were sensually rich and expressive. He rubbed his mouth from side to side, slipping his tongue inside when she took a half breath.

"You taste delicious," he murmured against her mouth. "And I plan on tasting every inch of you."

The vibration of his mouth on hers did things to her. She felt warmer, her face felt hot and her skin seemed ultrasensitive, hyperaware of his potent masculinity. He continued to kiss her, his caresses growing more aggressive. A shocking excitement flooded her.

How had that happened, she wondered. She'd been dreading this. *She had.* She felt his hand threading through the back of her hair, tilting her head to give him better access to her mouth. He pulled her against him and she instinctively clung to his strong shoulder, her champagne glass tilting precariously.

Leo pulled it from her hand, took a sip and then swore. Fire flickered in his eyes. "You're amazing…" He inhaled deeply, his nostrils flaring. He lifted the glass to her lips and she took a sip.

Setting the glass on the bedside table, he turned back to her and without a second of preparation, he pulled her shirt over her head. Three seconds later, he slid his arms behind her and unfastened her bra. Her breasts sprang free and he filled his hands with them. The sight and sensation of his tanned skin against her pale breasts was so sensual she had to close her eyes.

There was something primitive and carnal between her and Leo. She'd glimpsed flickers of it before and dismissed it as overworked imagination or hypersensitivity. He pulled off his shirt and his skin, molding to his muscles, glistened in the candlelight.

His strength, inside and out, called to her. She had been forced to be strong so long. What a temptation to be able to lean on someone else. And she suspected he was strong enough. She gave into the lure and slid her hands over his shoulders and biceps. "Good Lord, how did you get such an amazing body? Do you work out all the time?"

His teeth flashed. "No, but I have George to keep me in shape. I'm glad you appreciate it, since he beats the crap out of me."

He slid his finger over her bicep. "You do some working out yourself," he murmured.

She shivered again and his gaze slid to her breasts.

"Gotta keep up my delusion of having control over my life," she said.

His hands covered her breasts and she forgot what else she was going to say. He slid one of his hands down to her jeans and unfastened the top button. The sound of her zipper sliding downward felt as if it were magnified between her breath and his. He pushed her jeans and lace panties down over her thighs. She felt naked in more ways than one.

Her discomfort must have showed. "Looks like you need another distraction," he said and lifted the glass of champagne from the nightstand. He splashed some of the cool bubbly over her, shocking her with the chilled wet liquid.

"What are you—"

She broke off when his warm lips licked the champagne from her chest. Then he moved lower to her breasts. She bit her lip as her nipples grew hard and sensations swam to all her erogenous zones. She tried very hard not to arch her back, but her body acted out of its own volition.

"Good," he muttered against her nipples.

She felt as if her body began to spin. It had been so very long. She shouldn't let herself go. She hadn't in such a long time.

His hand slid between her thighs and he found her wet and swollen. Making a growling sound of approval, she felt him move away for several breaths. She began to come back down, but then he pulled her against his naked body. The sensation was so delicious and seductive she began to spin again.

"Leo," she murmured, wrapping her arms and legs around him. She wanted to absorb his strength, his passion, his life.

He swore under his breath. "Oh, damn it. I want inside you," he said and rolled on top of her. Pushing her thighs apart, he thrust inside her.

She blinked at the sensation, the thick, hard penetration of him.

A strange look crossed his face, and she couldn't prevent herself from wriggling beneath him.

He moaned and thrust again. The pleasure inside her grew. He began to pump. She clung to him, climbing higher and higher. Close, oh, so close, she was ready to burst free.

He sank inside her one last time, spilling his release in a long ecstasy-filled groan.

She bit her lip, still brimming with arousal, on the edge of a cliff, wanting to soar off of it. Something inside stopped her. Yawning need screamed inside her as deep as a cavern.

Leo rolled off of her, breathing heavily. "You weren't a virgin," he said. "You tricked me." A moment later, he rolled off the bed, grabbed his pants and left the room.

Calista stared after him as she tried to pull her mind and body together. Sexual need still hammered through her, clouding her mind. She felt as if she had no control of her body or mind. He'd taken both.

You tricked me. His words echoed through her mind. She hadn't thought he would know whether she was a virgin or not. After all, how many times had he had sex with a virgin? Her heart hammered with sudden fear. What if he annulled their marriage? What if, after all this, she still couldn't take care of her sisters?

Leo sat in the upstairs den with a bottle of scotch and bucket of remorse. His bride, the so-called virgin, had tricked him. What a fool he'd been, not wanting to seduce her lily-white sexual innocence from her. He hadn't wanted to taint her with his carnal needs in hopes that her purity would somehow cleanse his dirty past.

He chuckled with no humor. For a man who'd spent his youth deceiving others, he'd just experienced the biggest heist himself. He tossed back another shot of scotch. What was he going to do with her now?

The sound of a board creaking broke his solitude. He glanced up and saw her, wearing a white silk robe that belied her innocence. Her lips swollen from his kisses, her cheeks white and her eyes full of fear, she met his gaze. A surge of desire rolled through him. Lord, he was a fool.

"I never said I was a virgin," she said softly.

"You just inferred, suggested and did everything but say it," he said.

"You're not going to understand this," she said, crossing her arms under her chest.

"I can agree with that," he said, leaning back in his chair. He gave a cynical laugh.

He saw a flash of anger and defiance shoot through her green eyes, but she seemed to make an effort to quell it. She sat down in the chair across from his. "The truth is I had a sexual relationship during my sophomore year in college. It was a mistake. I thought I was in love. I thought he was the one. But he wasn't."

"Because he didn't have enough money?" he asked bitterly.

She narrowed her eyes and took a breath. "No. Because he lied to me and told me he loved me when he was involved with two other girls. That's when I knew I couldn't give myself that way again unless there was going to be a long-term commitment." She took another breath. "Yes, I made a mistake. Maybe you've never made a mistake. But if you had, then you'll know how it feels to want to make a fresh start."

He brooded over that for several seconds. God knows, he'd made a lot of poor choices. Who was he to hold this against her?

She stood and folded her hands in front of her. "I understand if you want me to leave."

His gut dipped at the prospect. "I didn't say that." He still didn't like that she'd deceived him. Part of the reason he had married her was he believed she was incapable of deceit. He'd obviously been wrong. A bitter taste filled his mouth. He hadn't been pure. Why should he expect anything in his life to be pure?

He downed another shot of scotch. "You take my bed for tonight. We'll discuss this in the morning."

She met his gaze and turned away. "Yeah, like I'm going to be able to sleep," she whispered and walked out of the room.

Calista stared up at the ceiling of Leo's bedroom with the covers wrapped tightly over her chest. This had been a disaster. He was bound to throw her out in the morning. Could she really blame him? He'd held off having sex with her because he thought she was a virgin and she'd let him think it.

She could kiss her sisters' future goodbye. She'd obviously mismanaged her charade. Calista wondered what she would do next. Would Leo annul their marriage? She couldn't believe he would give her a penny now. How horrid of a person was she to be thinking about money at this point?

She didn't want to think deeper than money, though.

She didn't want to think about whether she'd disappointed him. Or *hurt* him? Heavens, that had to be a stretch. The man was the personification of deceit. How could she even reach him, let alone hurt him?

Calista closed her eyes and counted backward from a thousand then counted backward again. Sometime during that second thousand, she drifted off.

In her sleeping but dreamless state, she felt the warmth of another body. A strong arm curved around her and drew her closer.

Her heartbeat accelerated. She rose to the surface of her sleep, and a hand slid over her hair, stroking. The touch soothed her and she drifted down again. When had someone stroked her hair? How long had it been? So long she couldn't remember…. She snuggled against the body that held her and sighed.

Minutes or hours later, she rolled over, encountering a hard chest and strong shoulders. Instinctively, she curled herself around the man and nuzzled her face against his throat.

"Calista," he said.

"Yes," she whispered, taking in the scent of him. She dipped her lips over his skin and darted her tongue out to taste him.

He sucked in a sharp breath and swore.

Feeling herself rise toward consciousness, she tasted him again, savoring the salt of his skin.

He gave her a gentle shake and she opened her eyes, encountering his dark gaze.

"Do you know what the hell you're doing?" he demanded.

"Do you want me to stop?" she whispered, her heart beating in her head, arousal surging inside her.

"Hell, no," he said and drew her mouth to his.

He kissed her and caressed and slid his fingers to her secret places, taking her to a different place. She wanted him inside her, craved his fullness expanding her, but he waited, taking her higher and higher.

She felt the tension inside her grow tighter and tighter. She didn't know if she could stand it.

"Give it to me, Calista. Give it to me," he coaxed, his fingers working their magic on her.

"Leo," she said, and suddenly she felt herself flung upward out of the stratosphere. Her climax twisted through her in fits and starts. She clung to him and he finally thrust inside her.

She moaned, feeling herself clench around him.

He groaned in response and thrust.

She arched against him, wanting to milk his response from him, needing every drop of his passion. He gave it and more.

Leo awakened the next morning with his bride in his arms. He felt a combination of cynicism and possession. He felt as if he'd been fooled. On the other hand, he felt as if he had gained a prize. Although she seemed innocent, he knew better. She'd come apart in his arms. Yet, even she had seemed surprised by the depth of her pleasure. That had given him enormous satisfaction. Knowing that he had taken her to new heights filled him with gratification.

Her blond hair was tousled over her eyes, her cheeks pink, her dark eyelashes fans against her fair skin. He suspected she didn't trust easily, yet she'd trusted him in marriage and in bed. That had to count for something.

As if she felt him thinking, she fluttered her eyes open. Her green eyes stared into his. She inhaled deeply and buried her head against his chest. "Good morning," she said.

He couldn't resist a surge of pleasure at the sensation of her voluptuous body rubbing against his. "Good morning," he murmured and exulted in her breasts against his skin, her naked thighs sliding through his.

She pressed her ear against his chest. "I can hear your heart," she whispered. "I can feel it."

There had been so many times when he'd been sure he didn't have a heart. He closed his eyes for just a second to drink in her essence then he used his chin to nudge her chin upward.

Her eyes met his, wariness warring with something he couldn't read. "Don't lie to me again," he said. "Don't mislead me. Don't shade the truth. Don't cheat on me. Do you understand?"

She gave a slow, solemn nod. "Yes."

"I'm glad we understand each other," he said and took her mouth and pulled her against him, determined to take her again.

After a night spent in Leo's bed, Calista awakened alone, feeling sore in secret places. She'd suspected Leo would have a strong sexual appetite, but she hadn't expected him to be quite so ravenous. And she hadn't expected he would make her so hot that during those private, primal moments she almost forgot who he was. She had the sinking feeling that she had gotten in way over her head. Grasping for something to quell her panic, she mentally flipped a page on the calendar. Technically, now that one night had passed, she had less than six months to go until she had completed her mission.

She rose from the bed and took a shower, allowing the

warm water to soothe muscles unaccustomed to such a strenuous, intimate workout. Drying off, she wrapped her hair in a towel, pulled on a too-large terry cloth robe and walked back into the bedroom.

The scent of bacon and waffles drifted toward her. She glanced at the balcony and spotted Leo sitting in a chair with his legs propped up while he read a newspaper. He wore a pair of jeans and an unbuttoned shirt that revealed his muscular chest. Her heart skipped a beat. She knew exactly how that chest felt against her naked breasts.

As if he'd heard her thoughts, he glanced up and met her gaze. "Good morning. Breakfast is waiting. I don't know what you like, so I told the cook to fix a little bit of everything." He lifted the large silver cover off the tray to reveal a feast of breakfast food.

"Good grief, that would feed a small foreign country," she said, her mouth watering at the sight of the fresh strawberries, blueberries and pineapple, along with the rest of the meal.

"What do you like?" he asked.

"Everything," she said, sitting down beside him. "I usually grab a quick bite or drink a breakfast shake before I walk out the door, so this is a splurge."

His gaze hovered on her. "No need to worry. You burned some calories last night."

She felt her cheeks heat. "So I did," she murmured and took a bite of waffle.

"Good?" he asked.

She nodded. "Delicious. Thank you. Don't you want anything?"

He lifted his cup of coffee to his lips. "I've already eaten."

After breakfast, she got dressed and Leo took her out on

his smaller boat. It was a warm, sunny day and she enjoyed the sights and sounds of the lake. He put down anchor in a private cove and she served the picnic the cook had packed for them, although she was still stuffed from breakfast.

In different circumstances, she would have been in heaven—married to a man who could take care of her and her family. A gorgeous, intelligent man full of passion with a sense of humor. She knew, however, that she didn't love him and he didn't love her.

"I need to take a trip to Japan in two weeks," he said. "I want you to go with me."

She mentally flipped through her work schedule. "That's short notice, but I'll check the company calendar."

"I'll be wanting you to join me on most of my trips," he said. "You may need to think about quitting your job."

She blinked at his suggestion and shook her head. "I couldn't do that. I work for a fabulous company with excellent benefits. I would be a fool to give it up."

"It's silly for you to worry about benefits now that you're married to me. You'll be covered under my insurance and I can give you an allowance twice your salary," he said.

Her throat tightened because she knew their marriage wasn't forever. If she gave up her job, she would be throwing away her future security. "There's no need to rush, and my company may be flexible. I would feel like a slacker if I didn't work at all."

"That's a first," Leo said with a crack of amusement in his voice. "I haven't met a woman yet who wasn't ready to dump her job for a life of leisure."

"Maybe that's part of the reason you married me and not the others," she said, lifting her chin.

"I doubt it," he said and pulled her against him. "But I'll give you a little time to work things out with your employer.

Just remember your first allegiance is to your husband," he said and took her mouth with his. "Always."

Calista felt a shiver of forewarning. It had been hard enough for her to hatch the plan of meeting and marrying Leo. He was such a strong man, inside and out, she wondered what she would be like after six months with him.

Two weeks later, Leo and Calista flew to Japan. Calista was still worried that she'd put her job in danger by insisting on taking the trip. Leo found her concern both irritating and sweet. She still didn't seem to comprehend how wealthy he was and that his wife would never want for anything.

Her brow furrowed as she studied her work assignments on her laptop.

Leo stroked that furrow with his index finger, startling her with his touch. "What—"

"You should relax. This is a long flight," he said. "I'm the one who has to be ready with facts and figures. You just need to look beautiful and act charming."

"Not quite. My boss expects me to have this assignment completed within three days. I'm sure jet lag will hit me before I know it, so I need to get it done while I have the energy."

"I don't know why you're fighting it. You may as well go ahead and quit," he said, turning back to his own preparations.

"I don't want to quit. I like my job. It gives me a feeling of accomplishment," she said. "I just need to learn how to juggle everything. I'll get there."

"We'll see," he said, shooting her a skeptical glance. "In a few weeks, we're going to India."

"India?" she echoed. "How in the world can I get off for two major trips within such a short time?"

"Exactly. Quit and I'll triple your salary," he said with a grin.

Not amused, Calista frowned. "It's not that easy."

"What's so difficult? I can cover all your expenses and more."

She hesitated a long moment. "I have some responsibilities with my sisters."

"I thought your cousin covered their expenses."

"They do as much as they can, but Tami has asthma and college is roaring toward us like a freight train."

"So tell my accountant what you need and he'll write a check. Money should be the last thing you're worried about. Instead, I'd rather you be prepared to meet my business associate and his family. My assistant completed a report for you," he said and handed a folder to her.

She lifted her eyebrows. "A report? I've been schooled in proper etiquette for at least a dozen countries."

"I know you have. One of your many valuable qualities," he said. "What you need to know is that you're not only meeting Mr. Kihoto and his wife, you may also meet his mistress, Shonana," he said.

"Mistress?" she echoed. "Surely he wouldn't flaunt that relationship with business associates."

"It depends on whether we go out to a nightclub," Leo said.

Indignant, she flipped through the report. "How am I supposed to pretend to his poor wife that her husband isn't a cheating jerk? Look, they have children," she said, pointing to the report, clearly appalled. "She's probably trapped in this marriage with an ogre."

Amused by her reaction, he bit back a smile. "I'm sure

she knows and accepts it," Leo said. "It's not unusual for a wealthy man to have a mistress."

She pressed her lips together in disapproval. "What's your opinion of it?" she asked.

"What he does in his personal life isn't my business," Leo said. "I just want to get the contract."

Silence followed and he glanced at her, finding her gazing at him thoughtfully. "Yes?" he asked.

"What is your opinion of taking a mistress for yourself?" she asked.

He laughed. "I have a beautiful, passionate wife. Why would I need a mistress?" he asked. "You're not worried, are you?"

She lifted her chin. "Of course not," she said and returned her attention to her report.

He noticed she fanned through the pages very quickly and wondered if she was truly taking in all the information. She set down the report and returned her focus to her laptop.

"What is Mr. Kihoto's age?" he asked.

"Fifty-three," she said without looking up from her screen.

"His wife?"

"Forty-five," she said.

"How long has he been CEO?"

"Twelve years. They have two children. A son and daughter. The son is oldest. He works for his father's company. He's married with a mistress too," she said, narrowing her eyes in disapproval. "His daughter is studying to be a doctor. No husband. No wonder," she muttered.

"Why do you say no wonder?" he asked, curious.

"With a father and brother who rule the roost and run

around, she probably would run screaming from marriage," Calista said. "Take control of your own life instead of giving it to a man."

Surprised by her reaction, he studied her carefully. "Is that why you don't want to quit your job?"

She hesitated a half beat, looking cornered and caught before she regained her composure. "From a personal standpoint, I gain satisfaction and confidence from completing my assignments with my job. Bringing that confidence into my relationship with you is a good thing. Plus, it's not as if we have children—"

Leo's stomach twisted at the mention of children. "And we won't have them, at least not for a long time, if at all."

She nodded. "I agree." She gave the report a little shake and shot him a considering glance. "It occurs to me that I know more about Mr. Kihoto, in some ways, than I know about you."

"Hmm. Really?"

"Well, aside from what happened before you were hatched at sixteen," she said.

"Life inside the egg was pretty boring," he said.

"I'm sure. But I know Mr. Kihoto's favorite food, favorite drink, favorite movie, and I don't know yours."

"Favorite food, lasagna. I had it a long time ago and I keep trying to find a restaurant that replicates the taste, but I haven't," he said. "Scotch or beer to drink, depending on my mood. Favorite movie, a tie between *Transporter* and *The Shawshank Redemption*."

She tilted her head to one side thoughtfully. "What did you like about *Shawshank*?"

"They were trapped, imprisoned, some were innocent. Morgan Freeman and Tim Robbins had to find their way to freedom," he said, thinking back to the days before he took his freedom into his own hands. It had required careful planning. He'd had to stick to his plan even when he was sweating with terror.

"You ever felt trapped?" she asked.

She had no idea. "Well, life inside an egg is bound to get claustrophobic," he said with a wry grin, pushing aside his darker memories. He was determined to leave his past in the past.

She nodded. "I guess we all have, at some point," she said and looked away.

He watched her, seeing another glimpse of the struggle between desperation and confidence. "When did you feel trapped?"

She bit her lip. "Mostly teenage years. A few times since then."

After her father's debacle, he realized. He wondered how much she knew about it. "What made you feel that way?"

"Family things," she said. "My father died and then my mother. My world turned upside down."

"You don't talk about your parents much," he said.

"Just as you don't discuss your time in the egg," she said, pushing back, clearly closing the door in his face. He didn't know why that bothered him, but it did.

"And now?"

"Now I try to depend on myself for my security," she said.

"Ah," he said, feeling another dig in his gut. He didn't like it that she didn't feel she could count on him, but he also understood it. Even though they were married, they didn't know each other very well. "Your job makes you feel more secure. In that case, keep it. Just negotiate more time away from the office."

She let out a sigh of relief, but he could swear she didn't want him to see it. One second later, her face brightened with a smile. "Favorite board game?" she asked.

"I haven't played board games in years," he said.

"Think back," she said.

He shook his head and strained his memory. "I don't remember much about it. This game had aircraft carriers and submarines and there was a grid and you had to guess the location of your opponent's ships—"

"Battleship," she said with a triumphant smile. "Bet you loved it."

"And what about you?" he asked. "What was your favorite?"

"In my younger years, it was Candy Land and Hungry Hippos," she said.

An image shot through his mind of Calista as a little blond-haired girl playing games. "And now that you're in your ancient mid-twenties?"

"Wii," she said. "I bought it for my sisters and occasionally whip their butts at bowling. I could probably whip your butt, too."

"Is that a challenge?" he asked.

"I'm sure you're too busy dominating the shipping business to play games," she said in a silky smooth voice, but the dare was still in her eyes.

"I might make an exception," he said and sent a text message to his assistant to purchase a Wii. "So what are the stakes for the winner and loser in your Wii bowling?"

She shot him a blank look and shrugged. "Bragging rights?"

He scoffed. "There's got to be more at stake than that," he said. "What's the use of playing?"

She laughed and shook her head. "For fun."

Five

The first thing that struck Calista as Leo's plane landed in Tokyo was the density. There were so many tall buildings tightly packed together. "They're so close," she murmured, looking out the window. She'd been so focused on her work that she hadn't had much time to think about exploring Tokyo while she was here.

"What would you like to see while you're here?" Leo asked. "I'll be in meetings most of the day and we'll have dinner with Mr. Kihoto, but there's no reason you can't explore. My assistant has arranged for a tour guide and interpreter for your convenience."

"I haven't even thought about it. What should I not miss?"

"Depends on how adventurous you are," he said.

"I still need to work while I'm here, but I should be able to sightsee a little bit," she said.

"Do you *ever* take a vacation?" he asked.

"Do you?" she retorted.

"Good point," he said. "You'll probably want to go shopping for souvenirs. The tour guide can escort you there. I have a few things in mind for you."

"What?" she asked.

"Surprises," he said and grinned. "You trust me, don't you?"

Her stomach dipped. *Yes and no*, she thought, surprised in a way that she trusted him at all. As long as Leo didn't know the truth about her plans for their temporary marriage, she suspected he would take care of her. But if he found out too soon... She shuddered at the thought.

At their hotel suite, Leo allowed her extra sleep to recover from jet lag. The next morning, she awakened to find him gone and instructions for contacting her personal guide. She got up and spent extra time in the bathroom, fascinated by the TOTO toilet, which actually lifted its lid as she approached and closed it as she left, all the while playing Mendelssohn.

She forced herself to work, although she was distracted by the beautiful small garden view from the window. After e-mailing one of her assignments to her office, she called the guide, a charming woman named Nakato. She went on a whirlwind tour, taking in the narrow streets, sounds and smells of Tokyo with a few shopping stops along the way. Nakato took her to a six-floor toy shop and she picked up a silly gift for Leo.

She dressed for dinner, fighting a sudden attack of nerves. When Leo walked through the door, she felt a whisper of relief until she saw his brooding expression. "How have your meetings gone?"

"Could be better. I learned that my biggest competitor

has already been here for a visit and Mr. Kihoto was impressed with him and his wife. I think Mr. Kihoto is a little put off by how young I am. At least having a wife means I've overcome one of his objections," he muttered under his breath.

Calista went very still, taking in his last comment. "Pardon me?" she finally said. "Did I hear you correctly? Are you saying you need to have a wife to get a business deal with this man?"

Still clearly distracted, he shrugged. "It's part of his expectations. My marital status doesn't have a thing to do with my business abilities, but having a wife smoothes the way."

"Are you telling me that you married me so I could smooth the way for your business deals?" she asked, shocked and almost hurt despite her own approach to the marriage. She couldn't possibly be really hurt because she didn't have any real feelings for him.

"I had several reasons for marrying you. I've demonstrated that," he said and flicked his gaze over her from head to toe. "I'll wash up and we can leave in a few minutes."

Calista paced from one end of the living area to the other, fuming. The more she thought about Leo's motivation for marrying her, the more upset she became. She remembered how he hadn't called her for weeks. He hadn't really had any feelings for her. He'd just been frustrated because his prospective business partners were reluctant with him because of his youth…and lack of a wife. So, what she'd really been was convenient. She wanted him to feel as vulnerable as she did.

"The limo's waiting," Leo said as he strode into the living area. "Let's go."

He took her elbow when they exited the elevator and she wrested her arm away from him. Despite the fact that she intended to divorce Leo in six months, she could barely swallow her indignation.

He shot her a look of cool curiosity as they got into the vehicle. "What's your problem?"

"You could have married just anyone," she said. "So, why me?"

"I told you before. You captured my attention."

"Plus I didn't want a big wedding. That was in my favor, too, wasn't it?"

Leo wiped his hand over his face in frustration. "Listen, there's no reason for you to pretend you're pissed off because part of the reason I married you was for practical reasons. You need to remember that you were very firm on getting married." His mouth tightened. "Despite the fact that you were not a virgin when we said our I-dos."

"I never said I was a virgin."

He lifted his hand. "This is nonsense. You and I have an explosive passion for each other. More than most married couples I'd say. You're getting what you want out of this bargain, and I am, too. If you wanted an emotional, romantic man, you picked the wrong guy. I never represented myself that way." He met her gaze. "Now, I want this deal. I don't want to feel like I've wasted my time by making this trip. So, just try to act like an adoring wife and you can resume your pissing fit after it's over. If it makes you feel better, I'll give you a blank check and you can shop off your anger tomorrow."

She stared at him in shock. "Do you really think going on a shopping spree is going to make me feel better about this?"

"Works with most women, doesn't it?" he asked as the limo pulled to a stop.

She would love to teach him a thing or two. After she secured her sisters' education and health care. She knew it was hypocritical, but his attitude still galled her.

"You're a jerk, but don't worry. I'll fake it," she said to him and got out of the limo.

Leo escorted her into the restaurant where a host greeted them.

"You're making a big deal out of nothing," Leo said under his breath. "Smile, darling. Here come the Kihotos."

The middle-aged couple approached and Leo made the necessary introductions. Calista smiled and nodded to each of them. "I have a small gift for you," she said to Mrs. Kihoto.

Mrs. Kihoto smiled shyly, but shook her head. "Oh, no, I can't accept."

Calista knew it was custom for the Japanese to refuse gifts up to three times. "Please do. It's very small and you would be doing me a favor."

Mrs. Kihoto gave a slow nod. "You're very kind and beautiful."

"Thank you. You're very generous to join us for dinner," Calista said and felt Leo's gaze on her.

When they sat down, he whispered in her ear, "Very nice. You surprised me."

She smiled, whispering in return, "Is this when you say 'good wife' and pat me on my head?"

She heard him smother a chuckle under a cough.

Calista successfully made it through the meal without stabbing Leo with her chopsticks and not pointing them in a culturally offensive direction. She even remembered to say the traditional *"Gochisosama deshita"* at the end of the meal.

Leo, again, appeared impressed. So did Mr. and Mrs. Kihoto. Calista collected her beautifully wrapped gift for Mrs. Kihoto and the woman also presented her with one.

"Oh, look at how beautiful," Calista said, admiring the gift. "You shouldn't have. Your company was a huge gift."

Mrs. Kihoto insisted and Calista thanked the woman and her husband again, relieved when she climbed into the limo.

"Very well done," Leo said. "I must show my gratitude. Since you're not interested in shopping one of my credit cards up to the limit, what can I get you?"

Calista leaned her head against the back of the leather seat and closed her eyes, the fiery brunt of her anger at Leo fading a little. She shouldn't have been surprised that his motive for marrying her was mercenary. And how could she blame him when her motive was almost as bad as his. The only thing that made her motive more honorable was that she was doing it for someone else, her sisters. Others might see that as splitting hairs. "I'd like a cheeseburger." She glanced at him out of the corner of her eye. "And maybe one of those TOTO toilets with all the bells and whistles."

He chuckled and loosened his tie. "Liked that, did you?"

"I was like a little kid. I think I played with it for thirty minutes," she confessed.

"I was the same way my first time too," he said.

She looked at him and felt a slight softening warring with her resentment.

He moved closer to her and pressed his mouth against hers. "You're an excellent wife."

"You were just surprised that I got Mrs. Kihoto a gift," she said. "I told you I'd been taught etiquette for several different cultures from the classes I took."

"True. I knew you were good. Just not this good," he said, sliding his mouth over her neck.

She felt a rush of heat despite her best intentions. He made her feel incredibly safe and challenged and irritated. He made her want to root for him. Probably part of his conman background, she thought cynically. That didn't keep her heart from beating faster.

"I'm taking you someplace the night before we leave," he said.

"Really?" she said. "Where?"

"It's a surprise," he said.

"No hints?" she asked.

He slid his hands to her waist and higher to her breasts. "What are you doing?" she whispered.

"Seducing my wife," he said. "Is it working?"

She felt as if she were melting into the leather upholstery. "Damn you."

"Too late. I've already been damned. But maybe you can redeem me," he said and slid her zipper down the back of her dress.

After a few days of combining work in the hotel suite and sightseeing, Leo awakened her before dawn. She covered her eyes. "Too early."

"I know, but Mrs. Kihoto was so impressed with you that she wants to take you somewhere special this afternoon," Leo said.

She peeked out from her fingers. "What?" she asked

suspiciously, taking in the sight of the too-gorgeous man who had somehow managed to distract her from the fact that she was peeved with him, that he was manipulative and lacking in human emotion.

"She wants to take you to a temple and Tokyo's best *onsen*," he said.

The temple was fine, but her drowsy mind tried to summon what she remembered about an *onsen*. "Sounds okay," she said and frowned. "*Onsen*? I can't remember—"

"You'll love it," he said. "Everyone loves it."

She rose onto her elbows and frowned. "What is *it*?" she asked.

"It's like swimming in a hot spring," he said.

The realization slowly sank in. "The communal bath," she said. "I'm going to have to get naked with your client's wife!"

"It's not that bad. You'll enjoy it. It will help you relax for your surprise tonight," he said and gave her another quick kiss. "I'll call you later."

"Leo," she said as he walked toward the door, but he kept walking. "Leo," she called and tossed a pillow that missed him by a mile. Frustration roared through her. She'd just been conned big time.

Hours later, after she'd visited a peaceful temple and taken a naked dip in a pool with a bunch of strangers, albeit feminine strangers who'd been fascinated by her fair hair, she reluctantly allowed herself to be driven to a different hotel for the evening. She was surprised by the modest outward appearance of the building. "This is different."

"Yes, it is," he said and led her inside the boutique establishment. They were led to a beautiful suite with a huge tub and expanded bathroom, but no bed. "Where do we sleep?"

"On the floor," he said.

"Oh, goody," she said.

He chuckled. "Don't prejudge. Our dinner will be served in our room."

"Can I have a fork?" she asked.

He nodded. "Yes."

A lovely meal of fresh fish was served via room service. Padded floor mats were rolled out onto the floor. Champagne was served with the meal.

"The champagne keeps it from being traditional, but I thought you might like it. I figured if they brought margaritas you might spill another one on me," he said, taking a sip of the bubbly.

"It's very quiet here," she said as she finished her last delicious bite. "I like it better than I thought I would."

"We're not done." He stood and extended his hand. "Come with me."

"Where are you taking me?"

"You'll like it," he said.

"That's what you said about the communal bathing," she said, reluctantly rising.

"And did you?" he asked.

"It wasn't as bad as I thought it would be," she admitted.

He led her into the bathroom where the huge tub was filled with steaming water with rose petals floating on top. She glanced at him. "I already had a bath today."

"It wasn't with me," he said and stripped off his clothes.

She looked at him, unable to tear her gaze from his body. The light was bright enough for her to see every well-defined muscle. In the past, when they'd made love, the power of his physique had distracted her so much that she couldn't study him. But now she could. As he turned his back to her, she took in his wide shoulders, the V-shape of his waist to his hips, his tight buttocks and long strong legs. He turned a certain way in the light and she saw thin white lines of abuse on his back and lower.

She stared at the marks, but then he stepped into the tub and turned around to face her. "Well?" he asked.

Rising to her feet, she pulled off her clothes. "I've already bathed three times today. I guess one more time won't hurt." She walked to the large steaming tub with the rose petals fanning away from the wake he'd caused.

He took her hand to steady her and she stepped inside, blowing a quick puff of air from her mouth. "Hot," she said.

"You'll get used to it," he said and pulled her into his arms. His nakedness felt delicious against hers. He was so hard where she was so soft. Pulling her down to her knees, he supported her.

"Yikes," she whispered at the heat.

"A little further," he said, splashing water over her shoulders. "Come on. A few minutes and you'll wish it were warmer."

"I don't think so," she said, but she allowed him to pull her the rest of the way into the tub.

He kissed her, taking her soft gasp into his mouth. She closed her eyes and the combination of the hot water and his naked body surrounding her made her feel as if she'd entered another dimension. She lifted her hands to his shoulders, her breasts rubbing against his chest. He nudged her thighs apart, wrapping her legs around his back so that she sat on his lap.

"Good?" he asked, rubbing his forehead against hers.

"Yes," she said, deciding she could let down her guard for just tonight. She was far from her sisters, far from her job and in the arms of a strong, strong man. "Very good."

Leo fed his bride a breakfast of fish, which she appeared to enjoy. After they'd made love last night, she'd slept like the dead. She often seemed as if a part of her was on guard, but he'd sensed something different in her. The woman usually seemed to be wound tighter than a clock, and damn if it wasn't his pleasure to unwind her. He watched her take her last bite and sigh with pleasure, similar to the way she sighed when he made love to her. Similar, but not the same.

"That was wonderful," she said.

"Good," he said. "Did it make up for your communal bath yesterday?"

"I'll tell you the truth. The communal bath was actually very nice and Mrs. Kihoto made it seem like the most natural thing in the world. She chatted and was very friendly." She paused and shot him a curious look. "Have you taken a communal bath with Mr. Kihoto?"

He nodded. "Last time I was here. It wasn't a big deal. Men aren't as hung up about their bodies as women are."

"That sounded sexist," she said.

"There are differences between men and women. Most of them are good," he said.

"Oh, really?" she said, lifting her chin.

He touched her pert nose. "You look snooty when you do that. Did you learn that expression in your girlie classes?"

"Girlie classes," she echoed. "You mean my etiquette classes."

He shrugged. "There weren't any guys in your class, were there?"

"No," she conceded. "I thought the classes were a waste of time the first two times I took them."

He stared at her, choking on his coffee. "How many times did you take them?"

"Four," she said with an expression of disgust. "I flunked them the first two times and my mother wanted to make sure I learned everything, so she made me take them a third time. Then I took the advanced level. I didn't want to take them again, so I got those right the first time."

He took another sip of coffee and watched the sunlight gleaming on her tousled hair. "You fought being civilized," he said.

Her lips twitched. "I wouldn't have put it that way." She rested her chin in her hands and studied him thoughtfully. "I want to ask you about something."

"Then ask."

She took a deep breath and frowned. "You have marks on your back. Were you injured at some time?"

Leo immediately pulled back. "Car accident when I was little."

Her eyes wrinkled in concern. "I'm sorry."

"I don't remember anything about it or anything before then."

"Oh," she said, a stunned expression on her face.

He could see the sympathy coming and was determined to stop it. "That was all before the egg," he said.

She didn't smile in return. In fact, she frowned. "Do you know how old you were?"

"Around eight," he said. "It doesn't matter."

"How can you say that? Don't you think it had an impact upon you?" she asked.

There'd been years when he'd fantasized about the family he must have had before the accident. Before Lilah and Clyde had rescued him. He knew his family had died in the crash, but he hadn't known how many siblings, if any, he'd had. He didn't know what his mother and father were like, if they'd treated him well. Now that he was grown, he suspected he'd been treated better by his real parents. How could he not have been?

"I don't focus on the past," he said. "I focus on the future."

"You don't think you can learn important things from your past," she said.

"I've learned everything I need to learn from my past. I don't dwell on what happened when I was child because if I did, I'd go crazy." He paused a half beat, refusing to give into the secret need for information about so many unanswered questions about himself. It was a fruitless endeavor. "We're flying out tonight. I've arranged for your guide to take you souvenir shopping one more time while I wrap up my last meeting with Mr. Kihoto. In the meantime, don't forget the trip to India in a few weeks. Have you cleared it with your boss?"

"I thought I would finish this trip before I start asking about another," she said, irritation leaking into her expression. "Are you sure it's necessary for me—"

"Absolutely sure," he said, standing. He was much more comfortable with her irritation than the sympathy he'd glimpsed.

She followed him to his feet, her irritation turning to anger. "And what if I can't?"

"If you can't find a way, then I'll help you," he said.

"That sounds like a threat," she said.

"No. It's a promise of assistance. Don't argue about this anymore," he said and headed for the bathroom.

"If you think you've married a submissive little Stepford wife, you are very mistaken."

He paused, thinking about her words. He turned to face her. "I never received any indication that you were submissive. I just understood that you were a reasonable adult willing to make the adjustments necessary in our marriage."

"And what adjustments will you be making?" she asked, crossing her arms over her chest.

"Whatever adjustments I make, they won't include continuing petty debates like this." He entered the bath and closed the door behind him, but not before he heard her make a sound of utter frustration.

Leo avoided her after that. It was amazing how much space the man could create around himself even in his personal jet. After they landed and returned to his condo, they might as well have been separated by a small city. *Fine*, she thought. She didn't mind. Every hour that passed when she didn't have to deal with Mr. Demanding was one less hour on her six-month time clock. His remoteness didn't bother her for at least two days. She had plenty of work to do. She visited her sisters and cousin and delivered the souvenirs from Japan and avoided her cousin's questions about her marriage.

The more she thought about what Leo had told her about the accident he'd had as a child, the more curious she because. On her return drive from visiting her sisters, she dialed the number for her P.I.

"Rob here. How you doing, Mrs. Grant?"

Calista made a face. "I haven't technically changed my name."

"Like that matters," he said. "Congratulations on bagging the big one."

She ignored his sarcasm. Rob had once wanted to date her. They'd become friends instead and he'd given her a cost break when she'd asked him to investigate the man who'd caused her father to go over the edge. "I learned something recently that has made me curious."

"What's that?" he asked.

"Leo was apparently in a terrible accident when he was about eight years old. He remembers nothing before that. Nothing about the accident."

"I stopped my investigation once I found out he was involved in the grifting scheme with your father," he said.

"Well, there's something about his childhood that bothers me. He won't talk about it."

"Probably because plenty of people would like to skin his late father and him," Rob said.

"Maybe," she said and mused about his response to her. "I probably shouldn't ask you to do any more digging."

"On your beloved husband," Rob said sarcastically.

"Okay. I get it. You don't want to help me. Can you at least point me in the direction I need to look if I want to get more information about his childhood?"

Rob laughed hysterically.

Calista frowned. "You don't have to be nasty about it," she said. "It's not like I'm asking for state secrets."

"I'll do it," he said. "You owe me drinks," he added and hung up.

"I can't take you for—" She broke off when she realized he was no longer on the line. Sighing in frustration as she approached Leo's condo, she slipped her key into the parking lot entry and tried to rein in her feelings. Her call to Rob had been impulsive and she shouldn't have made it. If Leo wasn't interested in his childhood, she shouldn't be either. Rob probably wouldn't find anything anyway.

Six

Calista's BlackBerry went off as she took her lunch in her office. Join Mr. Grant at 6:30 p.m. tonight for Philadelphia Business Owners dinner. Dress: business casual. Car will pick you at 6:00 p.m. at the downtown condo. Thursday night, George Crandall Museum for awarding of the LG Enterprises Scholarship Funds and Friday night Grand Celebration of the Arts on the Delaware River. More details to come. S. Miles, assistant to Leo Grant.

Calista stared at the text message from her husband's *assistant*. She shook her head. This wasn't even an invitation. It was a list of required appearances. *From his freakin' assistant.*

Her temperature rose with each passing second. She could barely contain her anger. Who did he think he was? Obviously, Mr. Important Leo Grant. Another text popped up and she strongly considered erasing it before she read it, but gave in to her curiosity.

Please confirm. S. Miles, assistant to Leo Grant.

She had two words for Mr. Miles and Mr. Grant and they were not Merry Christmas. Calista was so furious it was all she could do not to start screaming. Instead, she counted to ten. Twenty times.

She took a deep breath. First step, ignore the order. Second step, block Leo's assistant's number. Step three, work late and plan a long visit to the gym afterward.

Leo left the dinner early, wondering why Calista hadn't shown. In the back of his Town Car, he dialed her number, but his call went straight to voice mail. Irritation twisted through him. He wouldn't even have attended it, but the chairman of the organization had begged him. Little had he known he would be presented with an award for bringing new jobs to Philadelphia. The attention made him self-conscious. He was always wary of having his picture taken, especially if it might be put in the media. Even though he looked far different now from what he did as a young teenager, he always got a chill wondering if someone might recognize him.

He dialed her number again, but again it went to voice mail. Concern cut through him. He wondered if she was okay. It wasn't like Calista to turn off her phone. He was torn between an odd combination of missing his wife and not wanting her to ask questions about his childhood ever again. The conversation they'd shared that morning in Japan had opened old wounds he'd sworn to never revisit. There had been a time when he'd gone so far as to hire a private investigator to find out his past, but there'd been nothing except dead ends. Leo wasn't sure who his real parents or real family were and he'd had to face the fact that he never would. He hadn't wanted to claim Clyde as his father and was thankful he wasn't Clyde's son by blood.

"You're quiet tonight, Leo," George said from the front seat. "What's on your mind?"

"Regular stuff. I had nonstop international phone calls and meetings today. Barely had time to breathe," Leo said.

"Haven't seen your wife lately," George ventured, digging.

"We've both been busy since we got back from Japan," Leo said. "I have my work. She has hers, although I don't see why she continues. God knows, she won't need the money."

"She's a little more independent than you expected, isn't she?" George asked, glancing in the mirror.

"Yes, she is," Leo answered, unable to keep the irritation from his tone.

"If you'd wanted a tamer kitten from the litter, you shouldn't have chosen one with claws," George said. "She doesn't strike me as the type to take orders unless she sees a good reason for them."

Leo frowned. "Maybe."

"Odd that she won't quit her job. She's either very independent…" George said and paused a long moment.

"Or what?"

"Or she isn't sure the marriage is going to last."

The statement jarred Leo. He'd thought the prenup would hold her. "What the—"

"Just a thought. I could be wrong," George said as he pulled in front of the condo.

"Good night, George. Pleasant dreams," he said in a dry tone and got out of the car.

"You too," George called cheerfully.

Leo took the elevator to the penthouse and stepped inside. He stopped, listening for any signs of Calista. His housekeeper, Brenda, approached him. "Welcome home, sir. May I get something for you? A drink? Something to eat?"

He shook his head. "No thank you. Have you seen my wife?"

"Yes, sir. She came in about twenty minutes ago and went straight to the exercise room."

"Thank you, Brenda," he said and decided to fix his own drink. He went to his study and poured himself a scotch. Ditching his tie, he sat down and checked the overnight stock markets for a few minutes. He glanced at the clock and decided to head for the exercise room.

Opening the door, he spotted her running on the treadmill. She was moving at a fast pace and perspiration glistened on her arms and back. It wasn't at all unattractive to him. The way she ran reminded him of a cheetah in the jungle. She would be difficult for even the smartest, strongest predator to catch.

Seconds passed and she slowed. Gradually, she slid into a cooldown walk. Leo leaned against the wall and waited until she stepped off the treadmill and pulled out her earphones. She turned and her gaze landed on his, her green eyes widening in surprise before a twinge of anger came and went so quickly he wondered if he imagined it.

"Looked like a good run," he said. "Was it?"

She nodded. "Good stress reliever," she said and picked up a small dumbbell.

"Stressful day?" he ventured, walking forward, wondering

why in hell he hadn't insisted she join him in his bed since they'd returned from Japan.

"Still catching up from my time away."

"Did you get a message from my assistant?"

She wrinkled her brow. "I'm not sure. I got some sort of spam, so I decided to turn off my phone until I could contact my carrier about it."

"Spam?" he echoed, confused.

"It must have been. Some random guy I'd never met gave me all these dates and times I was supposed to make appearances."

He studied her for a long moment, but her eyes were wide with innocence. He cleared his throat. "Was the message from Samuel Miles?"

She frowned and shrugged her shoulders. "I don't know," she said. "It was so ridiculous I just dismissed it as spam."

Leo felt another surge of something stronger than irritation. "What was so ridiculous about it?"

She chuckled. "Oh, really. Think about it. If my husband wanted me to attend an event with him, he wouldn't send a message from his assistant. For one thing, it's incredibly impersonal. Plus the message wasn't a request. It was an order. Now that's insulting. And I just can't believe my husband would do something so incredibly ridiculous."

He was peeved and inexplicably amused at the same time. Her eyes batted in exaggerated innocence and he felt his lips twitch. "Point taken."

She met his gaze and took a deep breath. "Just so you know, I blocked his number."

"Whose number?" Leo asked.

"The person who sent me the spam," she said and lifted her chin. "I'm not your employee. I'm your wife."

He nodded. "In that case, wife, I'll expect you to join your husband in his bed tonight."

Her gaze flickered and she opened her mouth, but he spoke before she had a chance.

"Isn't that what husbands and wives do?" he challenged.

The next morning, Calista awakened after a night where Leo had pushed her to unbelievable sexual heights. She felt stretched and sore and amazing. Calista realized she'd never had a clue what sexual satisfaction meant before Leo. She wondered if he knew that, too. She glanced at the clock and dragged herself from Leo's huge bed. He, of course, had left a long time ago.

Stepping into the shower, she let the water spray over her, washing away her soreness and worries. When Leo made love to her, he took more than her body. He captured a bit of her mind, maybe even her soul. If she had one.

Rubbing herself dry with the Egyptian cotton towels, she returned to the bedroom and saw an envelope with her name on it propped on the bed. She picked it up, opened it and read it.

Would you meet me for lunch today? I have a charity obligation on Thursday and your presence would make it much more bearable. As it would for my obligation on Friday night.

He gave her his BlackBerry number. His request was infinitely more personal. Her heart twisted.

She typed her response. "Yes, yes and yes."

Hours later, she sat down to lunch with him at one of Philadelphia's most exclusive gourmet restaurants. "Thank you for meeting me," he said.

"Thank you," she said and took a sip of water from the glass that had already been poured. She looked at him, the man who had owned and occupied her body last night. "How's it going?"

"Could be worse," he said. "We got the Japanese account. I'm sure it's because of you."

"Not sure about that. Mrs. Kihoto made it easy. All I had to do was get naked in front of a group of Japanese ladies."

"Funny. Despite Mr. Kihoto's extracurricular activities, he respects his wife's opinion."

"Or maybe he just realized what a great deal you were offering," she said.

He flicked his gaze over her. "Maybe. What would you like for lunch? Anything is yours."

"Fish," she said. "I need all the brain food I can get. Especially after last night."

His lips lifted. "You flatter me."

"Not really," she said. "I just need to keep my mental energy going."

"Okay, salmon it is," he said.

Mere moments later, the waiter arrived with their lunch. Calista dug in, enjoying her seafood and focusing on her own meal rather than Leo. She needed her strength, her acuity. Heaven help her, she hoped the food would supply it.

She sipped from her water glass, refusing wine. "That was delicious."

"Yes, it was," Leo said, clicking his water glass against hers. "Would you like to go to the lake house this weekend?" he asked.

"I have to visit my sisters," she said.

"Bring them with you," he offered.

"Have you met them? I love them, but my sisters can be a royal pain," she said.

"So can you," he said, his eyes hooded with sensuality.

"Okay," she said. "But I've warned you."

She joined him for the events, dressing quickly after work. The first night he met her at home and made love to her. The second time, he took her in the limo. She wondered if she would ever feel normal again.

"This is kinda crazy," she told him as he held her in his arms.

"It's crazy in a good way," he said, kissing her.

"Are you sure about that?" she asked.

"Yeah, I am," he said.

Calista took a deep breath and deliberately drowned herself in him.

She felt him fold her around him as he slid inside her. She held onto him wanting more, wanting everything....

"I'm rolling onto my back," he said. "You can take me any way you want."

And she did, but at the same time, she was completely taken.

That weekend her sisters joined Calista and Leo at his lake house. Calista feared he would run screaming from extended close contact, but he managed. She was impressed at the way he handled them on his yacht. Then again, what wasn't to like about riding on a yacht?

Leo took Tina on an inner tube ride.

"Can I try it?" Tami asked, who was usually too cool to participate in what she deemed childish.

"Of course," Leo said. "You're up next."

After a few more minutes for Tina, Tami jumped off the side of the boat and positioned herself in the inner tube.

As Tina climbed on board, Calista wrapped a towel around her sister and hugged her. "That rocked," she said and glanced at Leo. "Your husband is the best."

Leo felt a surprising rush of pleasure at the teen's compliment. The appreciation he saw in Calista's gaze gave him an even bigger boost. Watching her interact with her sisters tugged at a long forgotten place inside him. Their teasing camaraderie reminded him of nights he'd spent wishing for a different family. He'd thought he'd buried those longings years ago. He couldn't help admiring the way the three of them had retained their sense of family even after all their losses and living apart.

"It does look fun," Calista said.

"You wanna go?" he asked, watching as her hair whipped around in the wind.

"Oh, no, that's okay," she said.

"You should try it," Tina said. "It's way easier skiing."

Calista shook her head. "No—"

"Oh, don't be a wuss, Cal," Tina said.

"More than one can ride at a time," he said, remembering Calista's traumatic experience.

"I'll go with you," Tina offered.

"For some reason, that doesn't make me feel more secure, *daredevil*," Calista said and bumped her hip against her sister.

"It would work," Leo said, because he could tell Calista wanted to go. "Tina could go with you and Tami could watch."

"Come on," Tina said.

"Okay," Calista said. "But you better make sure Tami isn't texting instead of watching."

Minutes later, Calista took the plunge with Tina. He watched her younger sister coach her on the location of the grips. He wondered how often the girls switched roles, becoming the teacher instead of the student. Despite Tina's bold personality, she was gentle with Calista.

Out of the corner of his eye, he spotted Tami lifting her cell phone. "No texting when you're the lookout," he said.

"Who's texting? I'm taking pictures," she said. "Are you ready?" she called to Tina and Calista.

"Yes," Tina said.

"No," Calista said. "Okay," she amended when Tina rolled her eyes. "Just go very slowly."

Leo eased forward, escalating slowly. Hearing yelling voices, he glanced at Tami. "Tina wants you to go faster," she said.

"What about Calista?" he asked, focusing on piloting the boat.

"She's okay," Tami said.

Leo revved up the speed and took a few easy turns. He heard a scream during the last one and immediately slowed, glancing over his shoulder. "Is Calista okay?"

Tami was busy snickering and taking pictures with her cell phone. "They both got thrown."

"What?" he asked, searching the water for them.

"It happened during that last turn," Tami said, still snickering.

Leo spotted Tina screaming with glee then saw Calista yelling at the top of her lungs. Although she was wearing a life jacket, he was certain she was frightened. Stripping off his shirt, he jumped in the water and swam to her. She seemed to be struggling for breath.

"Are you okay?" he asked, pulling her to him.

She gasped then laughed. "Yes, I'm just going to kill my little sister. She did some sort of spinning thing with the tube during that last turn."

"So you really are okay?"

She met his gaze and her laugh faded. "Were you really worried?"

"I remembered about the time you fell off the boat," he said, feeling foolish.

"And you thought I was panicking," she concluded in a wry voice. "Reasonable assumption, but no, this time Tina distracted me. Thanks for jumping in for me, though," she said and smiled. "Had enough of my sisters?"

"The three of you have an interesting relationship," he said, pulling her toward the boat. "Tami is busy laughing at you, while Tina is goading you into taking a spin."

"That's sisters for you. I'm guessing you didn't have any," she said.

He met her gaze and felt a strange twist in his gut. "None that I can remember."

She hesitated, looking at him and biting her lip. "That must be awful. Not being able to remember," she said.

He couldn't bear her sympathy or her empathy. It caused an ache inside him that no pain medication would salve. "Maybe it wasn't worth remembering," he said and before she could respond, he added, "Go ahead and climb on board. You need to dry off. Here comes Tina."

Leo piloted the boat back to the dock in silence, thrown back in time to all those nights when he wondered what kind of family he'd had, what his parents had been like, if he'd had siblings and if they'd died instantly in the car crash that had left him with no memory and a foster father who had abused him. He pulled into the dock, lost in thought.

"Thanks," Tami said and hugged him.

He saw Calista watching them over Tami's shoulder and hugged the teenager. "My pleasure. I want copies of those pictures," he said.

Tami pulled back and smiled at him. "Deal," she said.

"What pictures?" Calista demanded.

"Just a few of you and Tina in the water," Tami said innocently. "I thought I'd post them on Facebook tonight."

Calista cringed. "Don't tag me. I don't want my boss seeing those."

"Why? Because he'll be jealous you were having such a good time with two hot almost-college girls?" Tami said.

Calista groaned. "Just don't. And maybe I should send both of you to a convent instead of a university."

Hours later, after eating dinner and viewing a chick flick in Leo's screening room, Calista climbed the stairs to Leo's bedroom and washed her face and brushed her teeth in the adjoining bathroom. Then she crept into his bed, carefully sliding underneath the covers.

"Did you have fun?" he asked, startling her.

She froze for two seconds then took a breath. "Yes. My sisters had fun, too. Thank you so much for making this happen. I can't tell you how much this means to me."

"I'm glad you enjoyed it. It was fun seeing you with your sisters. It's impressive that the three of you put things back together."

Her pleasure in the day dimmed a little. Leo would be all too well acquainted with how her family had imploded, especially her father. "My father wasn't perfect, but he was affectionate and he made us laugh. He tried to teach me to play golf."

"Tried?" he said.

"Not my forte. He was one of the most encouraging people I've known. I would hit a ball all wrong and he would say things like 'You almost got it.' 'That's a good start.'" She shook her head, her heart squeezing tight with the memories. "For the most part, he was extremely optimistic. Maybe a little too optimistic at times, but I miss him. I miss his smile and his laugh and his bear hugs."

Silence followed and Leo covered her hand with his. "You're lucky to have those memories."

She glanced up at him. "You must have some memories of your parents."

His jaw tightened. "None I want to remember."

Calista studied him, wondering what was really going on inside him. He clearly had no fondness for his father. She prodded him with memories of her own father. "When my father died, I couldn't believe it. How could someone so vital and positive be gone in an instant?"

He met her gaze. "That must have been hard," he said.

She gave a humorless laugh. "Hard doesn't describe it. Nothing prepared me for hearing that my loving father could have died so quickly. It wasn't possible."

Leo remained silent and she felt the dark tension coiling between them.

"There was a man who tricked him into investing a lot of money. He lost it all," she said. "He went from being the most optimistic man in the world to hopeless."

A long silence followed. "People, even good people, can

get into bad situations," he said. "At some point, everyone wants a break. An easy way out."

She searched his face. "You sound as if you have some experience with this."

He narrowed his eyes for a sliver of a moment and shrugged. "Must have been all that time in the egg."

"What was your father like? After the accident?" she asked.

"As you said, I was hatched," he said and she felt him pull away from her emotionally.

"But you had a father, didn't you?" she asked.

"No," he said, removing his hand from hers. The gulf between them suddenly felt like miles instead of inches, or heartbeats. "I didn't. You should get some rest. Your sisters will try to wear you out tomorrow."

She sank into her pillow and watched him turn away from her. She'd tried to get her digs in about her father and she'd succeeded. She'd pushed him away. He wouldn't make love to her tonight. He wouldn't hold her. That was what she'd wanted. Right? So, why did she feel so lonely?

Seven

Calista's cell phone rang just as she was finishing her work for the day. She glanced at the caller ID and saw that it was her P.I. friend, Rob. "Hi. Did you find something already?"

"I need to ask you a few more questions. Meet me for drinks," he said.

"I'm not sure that's a good idea," she said.

"Why? Afraid your meal ticket hubby will complain?" he asked.

Calista didn't like his attitude. "You know about my situation with my sisters. I don't appreciate you mocking it."

"Okay, okay. I was just trying to keep things light. Meet me at The Mark in thirty minutes," he said.

"Thirty minutes," she complained, but he'd already hung up. Rob was an excellent investigator, but lacking in social skills. She closed down her computer and got her car from the underground garage then drove to The Mark, which was more of a joint than a restaurant or a bar. There was no valet service, so she squeezed into a parking spot behind the building and walked swiftly to the entrance.

Stepping inside, she glanced around and caught sight of him waving from the bar.

"Hey, Princess," he said, kissing her on the cheek. "Looks like married life agrees with you." He wiggled his eyebrows. "I'm surprised you haven't quit your job."

"Then you don't know me well at all," she said, perching on the stool opposite his.

"Not as well as I'd like to," he said as a bartender nodded toward them. "What do you want to drink?"

"Ice water," she said.

He made a face. "You're such a buzz killer. Loosen up, it's happy hour."

"I'm not going home with liquor on my breath," she said.

"Check," he said. "Don't want to piss off Mr. Mega-Bucks before you get his donation. What kind of prenup did you sign?"

She shook her head. "None of your business. You said you had some questions."

He nodded. "What kind of accident was your rich little grifter in? What year was it? How old was he?"

She shrugged as the bartender gave her a glass of water. "He was eight," she said, taking a long drink.

"But you don't know for certain," he said.

"No, I don't."

"Okay, well find out everything you can about the accident, how old he was, what kind of injuries he sustained…"

"He must have had a severe concussion. He said he can't remember anything before the accident. He doesn't even remember the accident itself," she said, thinking back to the discussion she'd had with Leo. "He has scars. His skin on his back is rough."

Rob gave a low whistle. "Sounds like you're getting to know him very well."

She sighed and met his gaze. "Do you have to turn everything into either an insult or a double entendre?"

"I do my best," he said. "Okay, okay," he said at her expression. "Just find out as much as you can about the accident and how old Mr. Money was when it happened."

"Okay," she said and took another sip of water. "I'll be in touch."

"You're going already?" he asked.

"Yes," she said firmly and slid off her stool. Just as she approached the door, two policemen burst inside with a dog.

"Don't anybody move. We're here for an inspection," one of the officers said.

"Excuse me," she said. "I was on my way out."

"Not now you aren't," the officer said.

Calista waited impatiently as the officers led the dog around to sniff at various people. They found marijuana on three men and unregistered guns on five. That knowledge unsettled her.

Suddenly someone yelled, "Fire!"

She joined the stampede for the door, nearly being trampled by the people behind her. She felt a rush of something cold and wet over her dress and winced. Rushing into the parking lot, she gulped in breaths of air as she ran through the graveled parking lot toward the back of the building. A bouncer blocked her from proceeding.

"But my car," she protested. "My car is back there."

"There's been a fire in the kitchen," he said. "We can't allow you any closer."

"How am I supposed to get home?"

He shrugged his huge, overdeveloped shoulders. "Get a ride or call a cab."

Calista groaned to herself. This had been a disaster. Even though she had George's cell number, she refused to call it. How could she explain where she was? She gave the host a big tip and asked him to get a cab for her. Ten minutes later, she sat in a smelly taxi heading for Leo's condo. She remembered he'd said something about working late tonight. She could only hope that she beat him home.

Thirty minutes later, she rode the elevator up to the penthouse and walked inside, feeling a rush of relief. *There's no place like home*, she thought, even though this really wasn't her home. At least she felt safe here. She headed for the refrigerator and filled a glass with water then turned toward the stairs.

Out of nowhere, George appeared. "You're home late, Mrs. Grant."

She covered her chest with her hand. "You frightened me," she said.

"Sorry, ma'am," he said and twitched his nostrils. "If I do say so, ma'am, you smell a bit like booze and cigarettes."

"I met a client at a bar. I neither smoked nor drank alcohol tonight." she said. "I was glad to get out of there."

"You need to be careful. A woman who looks like you. You need to be safe," he said.

"I am," she said.

"Good," he said, studying her again. "Philly has its dark places."

She nodded. "I know. Do you know when Leo will arrive home?"

"Oh, he's already home. Upstairs," he said.

Her stomach sank. "Thank you,' she said and climbed the stairs. She walked into his suite and found him dressed in casual clothes, working on his laptop. He glanced up. "Late workday?" he asked.

She made a face. "I had a drink with a client. Next time, I'll just be rude."

He lifted an eyebrow. "You could always quit…."

"Later. I have bills to pay," she muttered.

He frowned. "What bills?"

"College tuition, medical bills," she said, distracted.

He nodded, saying, "Why isn't my accountant handling that? I can cover that."

He said it the same way he could cover gas or a meal at a fast-food restaurant.

She shook her head. "They're not your sisters."

"My sisters-in-law," he said.

She felt herself weaken. Temptation slid through her. Wouldn't it be nice not to have to worry about money? Wouldn't it be nice to know her sisters were taken care of? That was her eventual goal, anyway. What would it hurt if he took over her expenses now?

"Quit your job and I'll cover tuition," he said.

Calista snapped out of her fantasy world. If Leo started covering her expenses now what if their marriage fell apart before six months? She would be unemployed and scrounging to take care of her sisters. "No, thank you," she said.

"Why?" he asked.

"Because while it may be fine with me to stop working right now, and I'm not saying it is," she added, "what happens when I change my mind and decide I want to work again?"

"That's fine," he said with a shrug of his powerful shoulders. "You'll just need to work around—"

"There's the problem," she interjected. "I may not be able to work around your travel schedule. Surprisingly enough, many companies prefer their employees not to take off at the whim of their husbands."

"Damn," he said, striding toward her. "And I was so hoping I could tempt you into a life of slothful, indulgence." He pulled her into his arms and frowned. "You smell like cigarette smoke and—" He broke off. "Is that cheap whiskey?"

"Probably," she said, trying not to feel nervous. "At the last minute, some clients insisted I meet them at a bar. I had water," she said. "There was a fire, so the whole place was evacuated. I couldn't even get my car because it was too close to the fire."

"Hmm," he said. "Why didn't you call George?"

"I didn't want to bother him," she said. "So I called a cab. I'll get my car tomorrow."

"What was the name of this place you went tonight?"

"The Mark?" she said.

His eyes widened and he swore. "Who in hell wanted you to go to that dump?"

"They'd heard it was authentic Philly. I suggested something classier, but—"

"Don't go there again," he said. "It's a wonder a gang

fight didn't break out. If you must go, then call George or me. Preferably me." He paused. "Promise."

She bit her lip. "Promise."

He raked his hand through his hair. "I really want you to think about quitting. I'll take care of all your expenses, your debts."

Tempting, but she knew she'd better wait. He could change his mind and she'd not only have her sisters' college expenses and Tami's medical bills, she'd also be out of a job. "I'm not ready to quit yet, but thanks for the offer," she said and he kissed her. The strength of his body and personality quickly slid past her defenses. Had there ever been a time when she could let go and rely on someone else? Count on someone else? In every possible way?

"You feel so good," she said, sliding her hands over his chest and up to his shoulders. She sank against him and sighed against his mouth.

She felt him slide his fingers through her hair and tilt her head to give him better access. He kissed her deeply as if he were making his mark on her, possessing her. "I don't want you going to dangerous places."

"I've lived in Philly for a while. I'm not a complete novice," she said as he slid his mouth over her throat.

"But you haven't been married to Leo Grant. That changes things," he said.

She pulled back slightly. "What do you mean?"

"I mean it's possible that someone would want to take advantage of you because you're my wife," he said bluntly. "I won't let that happen. I refuse to be taken advantage of."

She felt a chill run through her at his cold-as-ice tone. "I don't understand what you're saying."

"I'm saying I've never had a wife before. Never had

anyone at risk. I've had my security detail on call for you, but in the future, I'll make sure they're always close by."

She frowned. "Close by?"

"Don't worry. You won't notice them. They'll just be available anytime you need them."

Calista didn't like the idea of being watched every minute. "I can't believe I would draw that much attention. I don't need that kind of supervision."

"It's not supervision," he said. "It's security. You're my wife. It's my job to take care of you."

She stared into his eyes, feeling a passion as deep as her bones. It struck her in her heart. "I'm not used to someone watching over me."

"Get used to it," he said and lowered his mouth to hers. "You're mine now."

He made love to her, rendering her speechless and nearly mindless. In the back of her mind, though, she remembered that she needed to get answers from him. After the glow of climax, she curled against him, still breathless. "I don't know your birthday," she whispered.

He swore. "Why do you need to know?"

"So I can bake you a birthday cake," she said.

He chuckled. "November 3," he said.

"What year?" she asked.

"I'm thirty-two. Why are you asking me this now?" he asked, pulling her naked body against his hard naked one.

"Because I want to know more," she said. "How old were you when you were in the accident?"

He stilled. "Why do you ask?"

Her heart hammered at his still, emotionless tone. "Because that was a big event in your life. As your wife, it's important for me to know the good and the bad things in your past."

He took a deep breath. "I was eight years old. I don't remember anything before or during the accident," he said, breathing heavily in the darkness of the room. "I hate it that I can't remember."

Her heart twisted at his words. "Maybe it's best that you don't," she said. "Maybe it's too painful."

"I would rather have a painful memory than no memory," he said and rolled onto his side, facing away from her.

Deep pain emanated from him. She felt it in her heart, in her pores, and her stomach twisted at the power of it. Confusion twisted through her. How could she feel such empathy for a man who'd had a part in her family's destruction? How could she feel such a connection to him?

She fought it for several moments, but she couldn't stop her arm from folding over his chest and sliding closer against him, her breasts pressed against his back. She felt his heavy sigh. Did she have that much of an effect on him? Did she bring him a little peace? Calista marveled at the thought, at the possibility of such power. It couldn't be true, she thought. It couldn't.

The following morning, George met him outside the condo building. "Good morning. How is Mrs. Grant?" George asked.

"Fine, this morning," he said and climbed into the back seat of his Town Car.

"I can't imagine what clients would want to meet her at the place she went last night," George said, his disapproval evident as he drove down the one-way street.

"I have no reason to believe she wasn't meeting clients.

She said they'd heard The Mark was an authentic Philly landmark," Leo said.

"For gangs," George said.

"She didn't seem to enjoy her time at The Mark," Leo said.

George paused a long moment. "True," he finally conceded. "What are you going to do about it?"

"About what?" Leo asked.

"About her security," George said.

"I'm going to assign a guard to her, but I'm going to tell him to stay on the down low," he said. "I don't want her to feel infringed upon because of her marriage to me," he said.

George gave a rough chuckle. "She'll have to be the dumbest girl in the world not to know that her life would turn upside down because she'd married you."

"She may know that, but I also think she's fighting it," he said.

Silence followed. "Could be," he said. "What are you going to do about it?"

"This is a marriage," Leo said. "It takes time to trust. She will trust me," he said. "And soon."

"But will you trust her?" George asked. "*Can* you trust her?"

"You know I don't trust anyone completely," Leo said. "I've given her your cell number if she ever needs it."

"Okay," George said . "But what if I find out she's doing something you wouldn't like?" he asked.

"Like what?" Leo asked.

"I don't know. Seeing an old boyfriend? Or a new one?"

"She won't," he said, because although he might not have Calista's trust and complete adoration, he knew he had her passion.

* * *

Calista's cell phone began ringing on Monday morning.

"Congratulations," said a distantly familiar voice.

Calista didn't recognize the number. "Excuse me?"

"It's Jennifer," she said. "Your roommate from college. I know we haven't kept in touch as well as we should, but I thought you would call me if you got married."

Calista frowned in confusion. "How did you know I got married?"

"It's in the paper today—a little sidebar in the society section about how Philadelphia's most eligible bachelor has been taken off the market. Aren't you the lucky one? How did you pull this off?" Jennifer asked.

"We met at a charity event," she said, fumbling as she tried to remember how she'd described her relationship to her cousin and sisters. "It was just one of those things where we instantly clicked. I wonder why it just made the paper. We've been married for weeks."

"Did you make an announcement?"

"No," she said and realized that probably wasn't very bridelike. For that matter, she hadn't even told her coworkers. "I've been so busy…" She hesitated. "With Leo," she said with emphasis.

"Well, we must get together for lunch. I want to hear all about this. You were so studious in college. Never took time for dating when you and I roomed together. And now you're married to *Leo Grant*. When can we get together?" Jennifer demanded.

"I don't know," Calista said, reluctant to face Jen's questions. "I'll have to look at my calendar. My work schedule—"

"Work," Jen echoed. "You're not still working, are you?

If I were in your shoes, I would have dumped my job before the ink dried on my marriage license."

A beep interrupted her, signaling another incoming call. "Oops, I'm sorry. I have another call. I need to go."

"Call me back," Jen said.

"Hello?" Calista said, this time recognizing the caller as a member from her elite women's society club.

"You little sneak," Rachel said. "Why didn't you bring your husband to our event last week?"

Calista swallowed a sigh. "We've both been terribly busy," she said.

"But the two of you went to other events together," Rachel complained.

"Those were required of him," she said. "I'm sorry I can't talk now, Rachel. I really need to get back to work."

"Work?" Rachel said. "Why are you working?" She laughed. "Oh, Calista, we should talk. Better yet, why don't you and Leo come over for dinner? Would Friday work?"

Calista blinked. "I need to ask Leo first. He's in so much demand with his company. I try to encourage him to take breaks," she invented. "Thanks for calling though. I'm sure I'll see you soon. Bye now," she said and hung up and turned off her phone. Peace, she thought, breathing a sigh of relief. At the touch of a button.

She heard a knock on her door. Wary because of her previous calls, she rose to answer it. Three of her female coworkers stood there with their faces wreathed in smiles. "Congratulations! We're so excited for you," Susan said.

"I'm sure you've already given notice," Anna said. "Do you know who is going to get your office?"

Calista dropped her jaw. "No, I—"

Hal, her boss, a middle-aged man, approached from behind the three women. He shook his finger at her playfully. "No wonder you wanted all that extra time off. You told me you got married, but you didn't tell me your husband's name."

Calista smiled weakly. "We wanted to keep things quiet."

"Why?" Susan asked. "This is the most exciting news we've had around here in a long time."

Her boss's assistant waved as she approached the group. "There's a journalist from *Philadelphia Magazine* on the phone. She wants to do a feature of you and your new husband. Wouldn't it be great if they put you on the cover?"

Not really, Calista thought. "Would you mind getting her e-mail and asking if I can get back to her? I would obviously have to discuss this with my husband." Even after being married for a month, those words sounded foreign coming out of her mouth.

"When do we get to meet him?" Susan asked. "Do you ever have lunch with him?"

"Don't be silly," Anna said. "You know she's already resigned. Haven't you?"

"No," Calista said. "I haven't. I don't plan to quit."

"Why?" Anna asked.

That same question was thrown at her over and over. Between those questions and the incessant phone calls, Calista was exhausted by the end of the day and she hadn't gotten any work accomplished.

Hal glanced into her office. "Busy day?"

She smiled but knew it was more of a grimace. "Times two," she said. "Don't worry. I'm taking work home, so I won't fall behind."

"I've been wondering if it might be best if you take a leave of absence," he ventured.

"Why?" she asked, her stomach clenching in fear. "I know there was a lot of disruption today, but I'm sure it will blow over quickly."

He shook his head and chuckled. "I think you're underestimating the level of interest people have in your marriage. My assistant was fielding calls for you half the afternoon."

"I'm sorry. I didn't think people would care that much. I'm sure it will get better," she said. "Please don't let me go."

"I'm not firing you," Hal said. "I just think it would be in the company's best interest and yours for you to take some time to get your ducks in a row about all this. And who knows? After you're off for a little while, you may decide you like it."

Panic rose inside her. "I really want to keep this job."

"I hear you. That's what you want now, but it could change. At least, take tomorrow and think about a short leave." His lips twitched. "You're a newlywed. Enjoy the moment."

Calista fought the terrible urge to cry. Before now, she'd been able to keep her marriage under the radar. Now that the news had exploded, it seemed like that was all anyone wanted to talk about with her. It was hard enough to fake her commitment to Leo and herself. With everyone gushing congratulations, best wishes and curiosity, all she wanted to do was scream that the marriage was temporary, so it wasn't necessary to get all worked up over it.

* * *

Leo walked through the door of his penthouse after going a round with George in the boxing ring down the block. The former pro hadn't cut him any slack either. He would be wearing a nice bruise on his jaw tomorrow.

His housekeeper met him at the door. "Good evening, Mr. Grant. Welcome home. What can I get for you?"

"Bag of frozen peas, please," he said.

He watched her eyes glint with a combination of humor and sympathy. "George was feeling his oats?"

He nodded. "He won't be feeling them tomorrow, though," he said. "I got one of his ribs pretty good after he blasted my jaw. Is Calista around?"

"Yes, sir. She went to the fitness room a little over an hour ago," she said.

"I'll look in on her," he said, barely waiting a moment before Brenda returned with the bag of peas. Immediately applying it to his jaw, he walked to the fitness room and saw Calista pacing from one end of the room to the other with a frown on her face.

"Bad day?" he asked.

Her head shot up and she met his gaze, not smiling. "It could have been better. It started out with my car getting towed from the parking lot of The Mark even though they wouldn't let me get to it last night."

"Did you call George?"

"No. I picked it up myself after work, which brings me to another subject," she said.

Irritation trickled through him. "I told you to call George if you needed help."

"Trust me. Picking up my car was cake compared to the rest of my day. Did you happen to see the newspaper this morning?"

Realization shot through him. "Oh, the little piece in the *Inquirer*. My assistant told me about it. I don't usually read the social column."

"How many calls did you get about it?"

He shrugged. "I don't know. My assistant screens my calls, and he knows I like my privacy."

"I could have used that kind of assistant today," she muttered.

"Do you want one?" he asked.

"No," she wailed. "I just don't want all these people calling me. My boss even suggested I take a leave of absence."

"I don't suppose this is a good time to say Hoo-rah," he said.

She shot him a dark look. "It isn't. For the most part, our relationship has been between you and me. We went out in public those few times last week, but I had no idea people would be so interested."

He shrugged. "People are interested in anything that involves money."

"I'd like to say that I disagree, but I can't," she said.

"What are you going to do?" he asked.

"I don't know," she said. "It was really disruptive at work today."

"So leave," he said. "Let me take care of your bills. They can't be that bad."

He watched her stiffen in response.

"I'm accustomed to taking care of myself," she said.

"You can take care of yourself, but it's not necessary to take care of your bills. I have more than enough to do that. I wish you wouldn't slam your head into the wall about it," he said.

"Easy for you to say. I guess this means I can make the India trip with no problem," she said.

"I've put that off. The son of the man I'm dealing with is getting married. His father is distracted," Leo said.

"Oh," she said.

"Yeah, oh," he said, extending his hand. "What's it going to take for you to relax?"

She lifted her chin, and he was drawn to the pride she took in herself and her choices. "What's it going to take for *you* to relax?"

He gave a low, dirty chuckle. "Never gonna happen," he said and pulled her against him. "But I'll cover you. Relax."

For a second, she looked as if she believed him, but then her eyes flickered. "You need to remember that I try not to count on anyone."

"I'm different," he said and pressed his mouth against hers.

"I'm starting to think you are," she whispered.

Her body felt delicious against his. She would feel even more delicious when he was sinking inside her. "I'll take care of you."

"I don't expect you to," she protested.

"Let me," he said, pulling her off her feet and into his arms. "Let me." He carried her into the master bath and made love to her.

Eight

Calista awakened each day the next week feeling a surge of panic. She should be working. She shouldn't relax. She needed to be earning money because, after all, her marriage to Leo could end before the six-month mark if he found out the truth about her. If that happened, she would be out of a job and her sisters would be without the funds for their education.

Calista cleaned their suite, then searched for things to do. Leo's housekeeper, Brenda, repeatedly approached her. "What can I do for you?" she asked. "How can I help you? You seem troubled."

"I'm unaccustomed to not working," Calista told her. "I don't know what to do with myself."

Brenda laughed in sympathy. "You're the only woman I know who has trouble relaxing."

"I feel like I should be doing something," Calista said.

"You are," Brenda said. "You're Mr. Grant's wife."

Calista tamped down another surge of panic. "I guess," she whispered.

"You need to let me do my job so you can do yours," Brenda said.

When Leo arrived home that evening, Calista laced and unlaced her fingers. "How was your day?" she asked, but her mind refused to let her listen to his answer.

Leo snapped his fingers in front of her face. "Calista. Earth to Calista."

"Sorry," she said. "My lack of a job is driving me insane."

His lips twitched. "Then spend more time volunteering."

She took a sip of wine and thought for a long moment. "Hmm."

He lifted his eyebrows in enquiry.

"The dog shelter—" She broke off. "That's it. I'll spend more time at the dog shelter. Thank you for the suggestion."

He swallowed a chuckle. "Glad I could help."

Two days later, she brought home a dog of indeterminate breeding. He could have been part bulldog and retriever or part Lab and cocker. The good news was that he was neutered. The bad news was that he was a puppy and liked to dig. She named him Pooh.

"Pooh?" Leo echoed in dismay, staring at the ugliest dog he'd ever seen. "But he's a dog."

"I didn't know what else to call him, so I decided to name him after my favorite Winnie-the-Pooh animal," she said, rubbing the puppy.

"But Pooh is a bear," he said.

"It's actually a compliment. Pooh is an animal with a big heart and big courage," she said earnestly.

"That's still weird as hell," he said, feeling a strange tug toward the animal. An overwhelming sense of longing twisted through him. He'd never had a pet when he'd lived with Clyde and Lilah, but he had a strange feeling that he'd had pets before. It was odd as hell.

"Does he have his shots? Does he have a leash?"

She lifted the leash and smiled. "I would have sworn you wouldn't be the least bit concerned about a dog."

"I wonder if he can catch a Frisbee."

She snickered. "Agility trials, here we come."

He met her gaze. "I have to help him overcome his name."

That night, they taught Pooh to catch a tennis ball in his mouth. Or Pooh just knew how to catch a tennis ball in his mouth.

Calista laughed in exhilaration beside him. "He's so fun."

"Yeah," Leo said and tossed another ball into the air in the game room.

Pooh chased it, catching it in his mouth. The dog had feel-sorry-for-me brown eyes combined with a panting doggy smile and ears that swung from side to side.

"We need to take him to the lake," he said.

"Or a dog park," she said.

He wrinkled his nose. "We can go to my estate just out of town."

"It will be a hassle for you to drive into town," she said.

"Not with the helicopter," he said.

She looked at him and smiled, her eyes sexy and challenging. "That's an awful lot of trouble just for a dog."

He gave a heavy put-upon sigh. "Since you've already committed us, we have to do the right thing."

She clutched his collar and pulled him against her. "You're a sucker," she whispered.

"Only when I want to be," he warned her.

"I like that about you," she said and pressed her mouth against his.

A week later, Rob called her. "I have info."

"What kind of info?" she asked.

"Important info. You gotta buy me a drink for this," he said. "You gotta buy me a lot of drinks. Meet me at The Mark," he said.

"No way," she said. "The last time I was there, the police raided the place, there was a fire and my car was impounded. Pick somewhere else."

"Man, you've gotten snooty since you married a gajillionaire," he said.

"Be reasonable," she said.

"Okay, you want snooty. How about the top of the Liberty Hotel?" he asked.

She bit her lip. "You don't know the meaning of the word discreet, do you?"

"You didn't want The Mark. This one's on you. Meet me tonight at six," he said and hung up.

Calista stared at her cell phone and scowled. How could she explain her absence from dinner? How could she explain her need to be away at that particular time? She sighed, but was determined to get answers. She would tell Leo's assistant that she wouldn't meet him for dinner tonight because she was shopping.

She went to the bar and waited. Ordering water, she waited and waited. She dialed Rob's number, but there was no answer. She waited for another hour then left.

Calista drove home because she didn't want George to know where she'd been. She swept inside the house and Pooh raced toward her, jumping up on her. The dog was a salve to her guilt. She rubbed Pooh's face.

"How was your shopping?" Leo asked, strolling toward her.

"Good," she said. "Good. How was your day?" she asked deflecting his question.

"Busy, as usual. Where are your dresses?" he asked.

She panicked for a few seconds. "They need to be altered."

He gave a slow nod. "Okay."

"Yes." She rubbed behind Pooh's ears. "How much trouble has he caused?"

"No more than you," he said.

She made a face at him. "I turned down three more invitations to dinner and sent regrets for more charity events. I unblocked your assistant, and he sent me a text message today that since we're not giving interviews we should make an appearance at something. Do you have a preference?"

"Something where we can leave early," he said.

She laughed at his dry tone. "Okay, I think my women's society club is holding a summer soiree scavenger party soon. I initially sent regrets, but the organizer keeps calling."

"Scavenger party?" he asked.

"It's creative," she said defensively.

He paused a half beat. "Can't deny that. Call your friend and confirm."

"There's also a Saturday Expand-my-brain volunteer workshop for people of all ages in a few weeks. They want people with all kinds of skills," she said.

"I have no idea how I could help in that situation," he said.

She smiled. "You underestimate yourself."

That night, he made love to her with more passion than he had before. He consumed her from head to toe, making her sated, but still hungry. When he finally sank inside her, she quivered around him, milking him with her wet, feminine secrets until he shot to the top.

For all the times he'd taken her, he still didn't feel married to her. He felt an incredible connection to her, yet, at the same time still separate. Being with her conjured up feelings he didn't understand, feelings he wasn't sure he wanted. She panted the same way he did. Her breath mingled with his.

"That was pretty amazing," she said, sliding her hands down his arms and searching his face. "What—"

"You," he said, "inspire me."

Her mouth curved into a smile. "Who? Me?"

"Yeah," he said, sliding off of her and pulling her against him. "You."

Within minutes, he drifted off to sleep. Visions drifted through his mind. He saw a dog with a wagging tail, little boys with dark hair and dark eyes. A woman scolded him. A man laughed, his joy evident.

He and the other boys ran to the dinner table. He beat one of the older ones and sat down to a plate of lasagna. The aroma of beef and sausage made his stomach growl. He took a bite. It was the richest, most delicious pasta dish he'd ever tasted.

"Leo, slow down. You'll make yourself sick," the woman said.

The man laughed again. "Don't worry. The boy has an appetite. Hunger is a good thing."

Leo woke up in a cold sweat. He sat straight up, panting, trying to make sense of his dream. The images tumbled through him again. He felt a hand on his arm. Calista's.

"What is it?" she asked in a groggy voice. "What's wrong?"

"Nothing," he said. "A strange dream."

"Hmm," she said. "A nightmare?"

"No," he said. "Just a dream." But he wondered because it had seemed so real, so very real. He slowly laid back down and took several deep breaths. Forcing his eyes closed, he saw the images he'd glimpsed earlier. He wondered if they were real or if they were wishes. Or if they held clues to his life before Clyde and Lilah.

Family? A father and mother? Brothers? Was it possible?

On Saturday, Calista dressed in jeans and a blouse to attend the expand-my-brain volunteer workshop. She found Leo, who had risen hours earlier, in his home office. For just a second she watched him, allowing her mind to play with the idea that he was her husband. If there'd been no ugly past between them, she wondered what would have happened between them, what could have happened. Her stomach twisted and she shook off her thoughts. She couldn't undo the past. "Are you ready to expand some brains?"

He flashed her a doubtful look. "I'm not sure I'm the best man for this job."

"Of course you are," she said. "You're smart. You're successful. What's not to like?"

"You weren't completely clear about what we'll be doing," he said.

"It could be anything from reading a book with a young child to helping with math. It won't be brain surgery," she said, although Calista was certain Leo was intelligent enough that he could have been a brain surgeon if that was what he'd wanted.

"I may not be the best example for young children," he said in a stilted voice.

"Why?" she asked, even though she knew he'd tricked dozens of people and made money off of it. "It's not as if you're a crook," she said.

His eyes barely flickered. "No, but there's always my misspent youth."

"Hmm," she said, feeling her anger shoot out of nowhere. So that was how he described it. His misspent youth. She took a quick breath and counted to ten to keep from saying what she really thought. "Nobody's perfect. You have a lot to offer."

His mouth lifted in a half smile as his gaze fell over her possessively. "Are you speaking from experience?"

Her mind slammed back to visuals of their heated lovemaking and she bit her lip, bothered by the way her feelings for him seemed to jerk from one end of the spectrum to the other. "An observation," she said.

He turned off his laptop and stood. "Okay, but I can only stay for an hour or so."

Forty-five minutes later, Calista helped an elementary-age girl named Kelly with division while a crowd formed around Leo. She assisted Kelly until the little girl's attention waned and her mother collected her. Curious about what Leo was discussing, she joined his class.

"Whenever you're selling anything to someone, including yourself, you have to find out what the buyer wants. What does the buyer need? Your job is to give him what he needs."

"What if you don't have it?" a young man asked.

"Then you tell him where he can get what he wants, or prove that your product is the answer to his problems. The biggest part of sales is listening to the buyer and helping him see that you're part of his solution. How many times have you gone into a store and asked for help only to have a salesman take you to the most expensive model of whatever you're looking for instead of asking you questions about what you want and need?"

"But I just sell candy for my community group," a little boy said.

"Then you sell the experience of being a part of making the world better by buying one of your candy bars. Be what your buyer is looking for—a clean, well-mannered young man," Leo said. "Same thing when you're looking for a job. Do your research. Find out as much as you can about the company where you're applying. Be prepared. You can learn a lot on the Web. You may even find out something about the person who will interview you."

"What if I ain't got no Internet?" another young man asked.

Calista watched Leo, wondering if this question would stump him. He looked so magnetic, so self-assured. She wondered if anyone ever succeeded in making him feel self-conscious.

"The library has Internet," he said. "All for now. Good luck with your future sales."

She saw the crowd, both adults and children, push toward him. Everyone seemed to want to shake his hand. It was almost as if they hoped his magic would wipe off on them. She wondered if he'd learned his selling technique from his father. A bitter taste filled her mouth. He'd certainly sold her father down the river. Yet, even now she could tell that he wasn't all evil. He appeared as if he sincerely wanted success for each person with whom he spoke. Was appearance the operative word? Underneath it all, what was he really thinking?

He glanced up and searched the crowd, his gaze landing on her. She felt a frisson of excitement at being singled out by him. Yes, the rest of the world knew she was his wife. But she knew the truth. He didn't love her and she needed something from him. Nodding in her direction, he walked toward her.

"Let's go," he said and slid his hand to her back as he guided her to the Town Car.

"What is it?" she asked. "They loved you. They were hanging on your every word."

His body was tense, his mouth taut. "Maybe. They hear what they want to hear."

"What do you mean?" she asked as he opened the door to the car and followed her inside.

"Home," he said to George.

"Which one, sir?" George asked.

"Out of the city," Leo said.

She studied his face and instinctively lifted her hand to his clenched jaw. "Why are you so upset?"

He caught her hand just before she touched him. "I'm not upset. " He shrugged, his eyes dark and full of tempestuous emotion. "Seeing them reminded me... It brought back memories."

"Of what?" she asked.

He narrowed his eyes and shrugged again. "Nothing I want to remember."

She felt a strange twinge of compassion at odds with her wall of defense against him. "You gave them hope."

His mouth twisted cynically. "That's what I was selling."

"You don't believe there's any hope?"

"I believe in hard work, good timing and good luck," he said. "It's not easy being poor and wanting a better life."

"No, but what you told them is true. Selling a product, selling yourself, is a life skill. Don't you believe that? Or were you just telling them what they wanted to hear?"

"No," he said. "I gave that up."

She lifted her eyebrows at his revelation. "When?"

"Shortly after my time in the egg," he said.

"But you still used your sales techniques," she said.

"Yes. I found out what the buyer wanted, but I also found out that people believe what they want to believe. Some are harder to read than others." He lifted his finger to her lips. "Like you. What do you want to believe, Calista? What do you want to believe about me?"

Her heart pounded at the intent way he looked at her. She feared he could almost read her mind. She swallowed hard over the sensation of her emotions wrapping around her windpipe and squeezing. "I want to—" She broke off. "I believe that you're a powerful, charismatic man. I believe some part of you wants a family," she added impulsively.

He lifted his eyebrows. "Is that what you believe or what you want to believe?"

Her thoughts whipped through her mind. She wanted to believe that he was a bad person and that she should feel no guilt about marrying him for his money. She wanted to believe that she couldn't have feelings for him because he'd been part of her father's downfall. "I don't believe that humans are hatched. Humans are born and want and need to be loved."

His eyes bored into hers. "A word of caution. Don't overestimate my emotional needs. I've spent a lifetime learning to live without. I'm not going to start now."

His statement made her blood run cold. "Are you saying you have no real feelings for me?" she asked. "If that's true, then why did you marry me? Oh, wait, you wanted a wife to make your business deals go through more smoothly. So why me? Other than the fact that I was convenient."

"I told you that you fascinated me."

"And you thought I could be an asset," she said, digging into the dirty truth as much for herself as for him. She had to find a way to keep him from getting to her.

"Yes, but many women could be an asset."

"So all women are interchangeable?" she asked.

"I didn't say that. I told you that you fascinated me. I couldn't get enough of you," he said, pulling her against him. "I still can't."

Her breath squeezed tight from her lungs again. "You don't have an emotional attachment to me and you never plan to. What do you expect of me?"

"Everything," he said. "Your mind, your body. Everything."

She gasped. "That's ridiculous, and it's not fair."

"I never said anything about being fair."

That night, he made love to her, consuming every inch of her, wringing a response from her that surprised even her. When she awakened in the morning, Calista felt like a prostitute. What was she selling in order to secure her sisters' future?

Feeling suffocated by her feelings and her fake marriage, she took Pooh and drove to visit her sisters. With each mile she put between her and Leo, she breathed a little easier.

She brought a picnic lunch to share with her sisters and cousin's family on the back porch.

"Best picnic food I've ever had," Sharon said afterward when the girls and Justin adjourned to play a video game.

"Leo's chef prepared it. He's amazing," she said.

"But of course. The great Leo would have nothing less than amazing, including his wife," Sharon teased.

"I'm not amazing, but I get the job done," she said cryptically.

Sharon stared at her and blinked. "What do you mean by that?"

Calista waved her hand. "Oh, nothing. I was just joking."

"How are things going with the newlyweds?" her cousin asked.

"Good," Calista said. "Great. Being Mrs. Leo Grant means I have a full-time job of turning down social invitations, so I quit my job."

Silence followed. "You don't sound happy about it."

Calista laughed to cover her discomfort. "Of course, I'm happy. I can become a lady of leisure now. What could be better?"

"If you say so," her cousin said.

"I do," Calista said. "How is Tami doing?"

Her cousin lifted crossed fingers. "I'm hoping better. She's still hanging out with a crowd I don't like, but she's been getting home on time. I worry now, but she'll be leaving for college in the fall and I won't be able to do a thing."

"I'm so lucky you worry about her. I do, too. If anything changes and you need help, let me know. Now that I'm not working, I can be down here in no time."

"Thanks for the offer, but I *think* I have it under control." Sharon glanced around. "Where'd your puppy go?"

"Oh, no," Calista said, a spurt of anxiousness driving her to her feet. "Pooh likes to chew. We better find him."

Minutes later, they found him in the kitchen, his head in the trash can. "Pooh! Stop!" Calista said, pulling on the dog's collar. "I'm sorry."

Sharon giggled. "No big deal. At least he didn't make a mess."

"Good point," Calista said. "I should probably head back now." She gave Sharon a hug. "Let me say goodbye to the rest of the crew."

She embraced her sisters, and her cousin's husband and son. As soon as she got into her car, Sharon's words weighed heavily on her. Was it so obvious to others that she was unhappy?

Pooh panted beside her, making a whining sound.

"What's wrong?" she said, patting the dog. "Did you find something in that trash can that didn't agree with you? Serves you right for being a naughty dog."

Pooh continued to pant, standing then sitting, standing again and whining.

"Sit down and rest," she said. "We'll be home before you realize it."

At that moment, Pooh got sick. Distressed, Calista pulled off on the side of the road and cleaned up as best as she could. She put Pooh outside and waited while the dog got ill again. After several moments, she put the dog back into the car and drove to Leo's home.

She called her cousin. "I hate to bother you, but could

you tell me what was in your kitchen garbage can? Pooh is sick."

"Oh, no. I can't think of anything that should bother him. Let me see, there was an empty can of tomato sauce, an empty carton of orange juice. I threw out some old grapes—"

Calista's heart sank. "Grapes, that's it. They're toxic to dogs."

"Oh, I'm so sorry, Calista."

"I need to get him to a vet. I'll call you later," she said and pulled in front of the house.

She ran inside and Meg, the housekeeper, greeted her. "Mrs. Grant, welcome—"

"Excuse me, I need to find a vet," she said. "The one I regularly use is downtown. Pooh is sick. He needs immediate treatment."

Meg shot her a blank look. "I'm sorry. I don't know of a vet. I—"

"I'll check my phone," she said, panicked. "We need an emergency animal hospital. Damn this is slow." While she waited, Meg brought her the yellow pages. Calista grabbed the book and ran toward the door.

"Where shall I tell Mr. Grant you are going?"

"Emergency vet," she called over her shoulder and rushed to her car. Before she could open the door, however, she heard footsteps behind her. She glanced back and saw Leo. "I just talked to Meg. What's the problem?"

Calista felt a twinge of relief at the sight of him. "He's sick from eating grapes out of my cousin's garbage. They're toxic to dogs."

Leo shook his head. "I didn't know that. Let's get him to the emergency vet."

"But I don't know where," she said.

"I do. George gave me a tip just before I headed out the door. Give me your keys. I'll drive."

Calista petted the dog as she sped on her way. Pooh's breathing was shallow and his eyes were closed. Even though she hadn't had the dog very long, Pooh had brought her enormous comfort during the last two weeks. She was devastated at the thought of losing the animal.

Leo spun into the graveled parking lot of the vet hospital and Calista carried Pooh inside. "He's had grapes," she said to the receptionist.

Within twenty minutes, the vet was working on the dog. Calista wrung her hands as she was instructed to wait outside. Wrapping her arms around herself, she fought tears as she paced. She felt like such a terrible owner. She'd barely had the dog two weeks and look what had happened.

Leo put his arms around her and the gesture undid her. She burst into tears. "Oh, Leo. I didn't think much of him getting into the trash until he got sick on the way home. I feel so awful," she said. "And he's been such a good little dog. He didn't deserve to have me practically kill him."

"You didn't kill him," he said, stroking her hair. "And you don't know how it's going to turn out."

"I should have been watching."

"Stop blaming yourself. Maybe he'll be okay," he said.

Perhaps it was crazy for her to cling to him, but she had no desire to resist. Leo might not admit it, but he was attached to the dog, too. Pooh was something that had drawn them together. She could laugh and forget about all her complicated resentment and desire for him. He could relax and enjoy a pet. She suspected he hadn't had a pet for a long, long time, if ever.

Seconds later, an assistant appeared. "Dr. Keller has him stabilized if you would like to see Pooh."

The middle-aged balding man with the sympathetic face extended his hand to Leo and Calista. "You did a good job getting him here so quickly. I think he'll recover."

Relief coursed through her and she swallowed a sob. "Thank you," she said. "I feel so terrible."

The vet shook his heard. "These things happen. He's lucky you got him here so quickly. We'll keep him overnight."

"Will someone be here to watch over him?" Leo asked.

"Of course," the vet said.

Leo nodded. "Here's my cell number," he said, handing the doctor a card. "Call me for any reason." He led Calista from the building to the car and opened the passenger door for her.

"I'm sorry I was such a sap," she said, sinking into the seat. "I'm usually more pulled together."

"People get attached to animals," he said, pulling out of the parking lot. "Unfortunately when you get a pet, you set yourself up for loss."

Calista blinked at his assessment. "If that's the way you think, then why did you act like you liked Pooh too?"

"I wasn't acting," he said, irritated. "I'd have to be an ogre not to like that dog. He's affectionate and playful. I'm just stating a fact. When you get a pet, loss is likely to be part of the equation."

"You say that as if you've had some experience in the area," she said, searching his face.

He frowned and swore under his breath. "None that I can recall," he said.

Calista looked at him and felt a strange shifting inside

her. He was the strongest, most compelling man she'd ever met. For all that strength, though, she sensed a need in him, a need he would likely deny. A need she wanted to fulfill. Where had the urge come from? It would be incredibly dangerous for her to give into her feelings, but she was beginning to wonder if she could stop herself. She felt as if she were walking on a precipice, and keeping the balance was becoming more impossible with each step.

If she were smart, she would turn her head toward the window and continue to play keep-away with her emotions. At the moment, though, she couldn't imagine doing that. She reached across the seat and put her hand on his arm.

He glanced toward her.

"Thank you for going with me," she said. "I could have done it by myself, but having you there made it easier for me. I've had to do most everything on my own since my parents passed away. I'm not used to depending on anyone."

"You're married to me. You can depend on me now," he said.

In the back of her mind, Calista knew she shouldn't, but just for a little while, she decided to allow herself the luxury of pretending that she could.

Nine

"I hope you don't mind, but I really don't feel like a big dinner tonight," Calista said after Leo led her into the house. She liked the feeling of his arms around her too much.

"You've had a rough day. Take a shower. I have a few more calls to make then I'll come upstairs and join you in about an hour," he said. "I'll ask Meg to bring up some sandwiches for us." He dropped a kiss on her forehead. "Go on," he said and gave her a gentle nudge.

Calista took his advice and climbed the stairs to Leo's suite. Instead of taking a shower, though, she gave into the temptation to take a bath. She had an hour after all. While she drew the water in the large, luxurious tub, Meg appeared with a glass of chilled wine. Calista smiled and thanked the woman. A thoughtful gesture from Leo, she suspected. She stripped and stepped into the tub, sinking into the hot water.

Her mind racing between worry for Pooh and concern for her sisters, she turned on the bathroom sound system to Michael Buble. She told herself to stop thinking for just a few minutes. Pooh was in good hands and she was working on her sister's future.

Lifting the glass of wine to her lips, she took a sip and closed her eyes.

"Well this is a sight for sore eyes," Leo said.

Her eyes flashed open at the sound of his voice and she sat up then sank under the water, her wine splashing on her chest. A sound of exasperation bubbled from her throat. "Did you consider knocking?"

"Hell, no," he said, resting one hand on his hip while his other hand held his glass of wine as his gaze seemed to devour her. "It was so quiet in here I wondered if you'd fainted." Moving toward her, he set his wineglass on the side of the tub, and her heart skittered like a stone tossed across a river.

"I obviously haven't," she said, watching as he pulled his shirt over his head and unfastened his slacks. Seconds later, his boxers hit the floor. Had the water grown hotter?

"You don't mind if I join you, do you?" he said more than asked as he stepped into the bath.

"You didn't exactly give me a chance to refuse," she said, trying not to be fascinated by the width of his shoulders and muscular body. His physique was impressive in *every* way.

"No need to thank me yet," he said with a wicked grin as he pushed her into a sitting position and slid behind her.

"Leo," she said. "I thought the objective was for me to calm down."

"You will," he said, skimming his mouth over her bare shoulder.

"How can—"

He held his wineglass to her mouth with the silent instruction for her to take a sip. She did, but she didn't feel one bit more calm. "I don't see—"

He slid her slightly to the side and tilted her head upward. "Trust me," he said and lowered his mouth to hers.

Trust him? How could she possibly? He slid both their bodies deeper into the water. She barely noticed the sound of him placing the wineglass on the side of the tub. His kiss was so compelling. A half-breath later, she felt his hand on her skin, skimming down to her breasts. The combination of the warm water, his seductive touch and the sensation of her back against his body sent every thought but him from her mind. He taunted her nipples at the same time as he drew her tongue deeply into his mouth.

She tried to roll over to face him, but he pulled back, shaking his head. "Uh-uh, not now."

Calista frowned, but his hand traveled down, further down between her legs and he found where she was already swollen and sensitive. She gasped against his mouth and he kissed her again. She felt his strength beneath her, his obvious arousal against her, as he kissed her and played with her sending her into the stratosphere. His caresses made her breathless, mindless. Her climax racked through her from head to toe. "Oh, Leo," she whispered.

"Now, you can turn over," he said.

She rolled over and covered his lips with her fingers. "No, now I want you to stand up."

He frowned, his eyes glittering with desire. "Why?"

"Just do it," she whispered.

Sighing heavily, he stood, the water coursing down his strong thighs, his erection jutting proudly. Still weak from the way he affected her, she rose to her knees and skimmed her hands up his thighs to cup him.

He let out a sigh of utter sexual frustration.

Holding his gaze, Calista lifted her lips and took him intimately into her mouth.

He said things that sounded like a combination of curses and longing. He wrapped his fingers in her hair and shook his head, drawing her head away from him. "Enough," he muttered.

Heedless of their wet skin, he picked her up and carried her into the bedroom, laying her on the bed, immediately following her down. "Hold on," he said. "I have to have you."

He took her in one sure thrust. She gazed into his dark eyes and the power she saw there made her feel as if she should look away. She felt as if he were taking more than her body. He was taking her soul.

When Calista awakened the next morning, she felt exhausted. Leo had made love to her several times during the night. She peeked through her fingers and saw that he was gone. She felt a twinge of disappointment, but told herself not to be surprised. Leo was almost always gone in the morning. A terrible loneliness sank inside her.

Growling in frustration, she threw off the covers and rose from the bed. "This is ridiculous," she muttered. "Lying in bed like some pitiful, sappy, helpless woman in love. I'm not helpless and I'm not in love," she told herself and glanced into the bathroom mirror. She'd made a plan, and she was working the plan.

The woman in the reflection, however, told a different

story. Calista lifted her fingers to her swollen lips. Her skin was pale, her eyes bloodshot, her hair a tumbled telltale tangle. Worse yet, the expression in her eyes was full of sadness and longing.

Unable to bear the sight of her naked emotions, she closed her eyes and turned away, taking a deep breath. She turned on the jets to the shower, determined to wash her vulnerability down the drain.

"Calista," Leo said from the doorway.

She jumped at the sound of his voice, wishing she was dressed. Instead, she crossed her arms over her chest in a feeble attempt to cover herself. "I thought you'd left."

"Almost," he said and offered her a steaming cup of coffee. "I waited to talk to the vet. They want to keep Pooh one more night."

Concern rushed through her as she accepted the coffee. "Did something happen? Did his condition worsen?"

He shook his head. "No, I just told them I want them to make sure he's well. In that case, he said they'd keep him another night on IV support. We should be able to pick him up tomorrow."

"You're sure?" she asked, setting the coffee on a table inside the bathroom.

He shot her a half grin. "Yeah, I'm sure." His gaze fell over her body. "Now, you'd better hop into that shower before I decide I need to distract you like I did last night."

Calista didn't know if her body or her emotions could take it, so she quickly stepped under the spray. She didn't linger, reaching for a towel as soon as she got out of the shower. She lifted the cup of coffee for a quick life-giving sip and noticed it was laced with vanilla and hazelnut. Surprised, she felt her heart take a dip. Leo took his coffee black. He wouldn't come within an inch of her girlie cappuccinos. She wondered if Meg or Leo knew her tastes.

Bombarded with more social invitations since they'd attended the expand-my-brain program on Saturday, Calista sorted out the few possible events she thought might interest Leo. She also talked with her sisters and cousin, reassuring them about Pooh.

Her cousin came back on the line after Calista finished talking to her sisters. "I hate to have to tell you this," she said. "But I'm pretty sure Tami has been smoking again."

Calista's stomach clenched. "But that's terrible for her asthma."

"I know. I've told her the same thing. I'm not sure what to do next. You know that when Fall rolls around, she'll go away to school and neither you nor I will be able to say a thing to her."

Calista sighed. "I'm not liking this," she said. "Not at all. Do you think it would help if she talked to a doctor?"

"I don't know. She's a teenager. It's hard to tell her anything. I'm keeping close tabs on her, though. I've told her I want her to start bringing her friends here instead of going out."

"What does she say to that?"

"She doesn't like it, but I'm not giving her much choice," Sharon said.

"Thanks. I'll think about this. There's got to be a solution," Calista said.

"I just wanted you to know. We'll talk soon," Sharon said.

"Yes, we will. Goodbye."

Calista stewed over the news about her sister after she

disconnected from the phone. Tami should know better. She'd had plenty of frightening asthmatic episodes.

"Mrs. Grant," Meg said, interrupting her thoughts. "You have a visitor. Mr. Rob Miller."

Calista felt a dart of surprise followed by extreme discomfort. "Oh. Um. He's a business colleague. Last week, he told me he needed to ask me a few questions about my projects. Please show him onto the back porch. I'll be down in just a moment."

Why had Rob shown up here without any warning? Her heart pounded in her chest out of fear. How could she explain him to Leo? Her hands turned clammy and she felt terror chill her to the bone.

Taking a deep breath, she struggled for composure. She would calmly arrange to meet him some other time at some other place. Calista walked from her makeshift office upstairs down to the back porch and closed the door behind her.

Rob turned to greet her. "Nice place," he said.

She bit her lip, but kept her voice low. "What are you doing here? Why didn't you call first?"

"Your cell phone changed. I called your work number and they said you were on extended leave. Hey, if you don't want the information—"

"No, no," she said, her stomach twisting. "What have you learned about Leo?"

"It's not just about Leo," he said. "It's about your father."

"What do you mean?" she asked.

"I hate to be the one to tell you, but I think you should know. I also knew you shouldn't see this in a report."

Her heart hammered against her chest in apprehension. "What? What is it?"

He moved closer to her and took her hand, lowering his voice. "Your father didn't die of a heart attack. He committed suicide."

Leo decided to leave the office early. Despite their trip to Japan, he realized he and Calista hadn't had a real honeymoon. Although he couldn't leave his business at the moment, he thought it would be a nice surprise to let her choose the place. Having a wife wasn't such a bad deal after all. Remembering how she'd melted in his arms the night before, he felt a new urgency to be with her again.

Meg greeted him as he walked into the house. "Welcome home, Mr. Grant."

"Thank you, Meg. Do you know where Calista is?"

His housekeeper paused. "She has a visitor. She's talking with him on the back porch."

Him? Leo frowned. He didn't like the sound of that. He walked through the house toward the back porch, stopping suddenly when he spotted Calista in another man's arms. His stomach gave a vicious, sickening twist. The man caressed her back as she clung to him.

Who the hell was this? What was he doing with her? What was she doing with him? This was his house, damn it.

Taking a sharp breath, he strode to the porch and threw open the door. "Anyone want to tell me what's going on?"

Calista pushed herself from his arms, clearly startled, a guilty expression crossing her face. "Leo?"

"Yes, it's me. Your husband. Introduce me to your—" He paused. "Guest," he said in distaste.

She licked her lips nervously. "This is Rob. He was just leaving."

"It didn't look that way," Leo said, staring the other man down.

The man lifted his hands. "Excuse me. I'll talk to you later," he said to Calista.

She cringed as the man left.

"You want to explain what I just saw?" Leo asked, clenching his jaw.

She walked toward him. "It's not how it seemed."

"Then how was it?"

"It's hard to explain," she said.

"I'll bet. How long have you been involved with him?"

"It's not like that," she said. "I swear."

"Then why were you in each other's arms?"

She closed her eyes for a second then took a deep breath. "He's a private investigator. He just told me that my father didn't die of a heart attack. He committed suicide. I never knew," she said in a broken voice.

"If he's a P.I., then why the hell was he holding you in his arms?"

"I've known him for a while. He's a friend."

"Just a friend?" Leo asked, full of doubt.

"Yes," she insisted. "You have to believe me."

"No. I don't," he said, suspicion trickling through him like acid.

Fear and dread darkened her gaze. "Leo, you have to believe I would never sacrifice our marriage for a stupid affair."

"Why not?" he asked, challenging her. How foolish he'd been, he thought. He'd actually been on the verge of trusting her.

She bit her lip. "I wouldn't. I couldn't." She closed her eyes. "My marriage to you is too important."

"Because I can give you money," he said, goading her.

She opened her eyes and stared at him in shock. She took a deep breath. "Not for me, but for my sisters," she finally said. "Yes, I need the money for their education and for Tami's health problems."

"Is that why you married me?" he demanded. "To take care of your sisters?"

Her eyes turned cold. "What room do you have to judge? I know you and your father pulled a grifting scheme over on my father. I thought his shame had killed him. It turns out he took his life because of what you and your father did."

Her words hit him like a block of ice. He stared at her in disbelief. "You knew about my father and me?" He shook his head. "Why didn't you just threaten to blackmail me?"

She gave him a blank stare. "Blackmail didn't occur to me. I wanted my sisters to get a good education and I couldn't pay for it. I've been too busy paying off other family debts," she said bitterly.

He laughed, but the sound was hollow to his own ears. "You used me."

She lifted her chin and met his gaze. "The same way you used me so you could get the Japanese account."

"Sweet little Calista," he said in disbelief. "I never would have thought it."

Pain shadowed her eyes. "I never would have done it if I didn't believe it was necessary."

He shook his head. "How long did you plan to keep going with this charade?" he asked.

"Long enough to secure my sisters' future."

"Six months," he said, remembering the prenup.

She crossed her arms over her chest. "So now you see why I wouldn't possibly risk an affair."

"Your sisters," he said.

She nodded. "That and the fact that I'm not the kind of woman to go to bed with one man while I'm married to another."

He gave another humorless chuckle. "I'll never know that for certain. Will I?"

Another shot of pain flashed through her beautiful green eyes. He could almost believe she felt some sense of remorse. Almost. He could pay her and send her away. He could send her away and give her nothing. He knew, however, that he'd had a part in bringing down her father. The bitter reality backed up in his throat. At this second, he detested the very sight of her. But it was as much because she held a mirror to him of his past sins.

"Take my room tonight. I'm going into town."

She blinked in surprise as if she'd expected him to send her away. He wanted to. He wished he could, but something inside stopped him. "You can pick up Pooh in the morning." He turned and walked away.

"Leo," she called after him.

He paused. "What?"

"I—" She broke off. "I didn't expect things to turn out this way."

He walked out the door.

He'd fallen for the biggest con of his lifetime. He'd been so willing to believe her, so determined to protect her. He'd thought she could make him clean, and she had to the outside world. With Calista as his wife, it was easier for people to forget the fact that his past was murky at best. Her presence had greased the wheels for some of his business deals, too.

Leo had a choice to make. He could either cut Calista loose or hold on. He could make her pay for using him. He could make her life miserable, but he wondered if he would be making himself miserable at the same time.

This wasn't a decision to be made in the heat of anger. He needed time and distance.

Calista didn't know what to do. She sure hadn't expected to blurt out her reasons for marrying him. She wasn't sure if she should leave or stay. The thought of her sisters and unexpected feelings for Leo made her stay. He was more than she'd thought he would be. She did everything she could to fall asleep. Exercise, take a bath, drink warm milk.

She went to bed, turned out the lights and her eyelids would not close. Sighing, she turned to her side and forced her eyes closed. Immediately, images of Leo raced through her mind. Leo laughing, Leo concerned about Pooh, Leo making love to her.

A tiny wail squeezed through her throat. What was she supposed to do?

Leo was a successful man, a hard man. Surely, he wasn't capable of being hurt. Surely she couldn't hurt him.

Inhaling deeply, she couldn't tear her thoughts away from him. She felt a connection to him that went deeper than the volatile lovemaking they'd shared. A part of her hated that she'd destroyed the possibility of sharing a future with him. She'd never intended that, she reminded herself. Never.

She closed her eyes again and mentally rocked herself to sleep.

The next morning, Calista picked Pooh up from the veterinary hospital. The dog was groggy, but wagged his tail in welcome. Despite her distraction with Leo, Calista's heart lifted.

"Hello, you naughty, sweetie pie. You scared the daylights out of me. You better not do it again," she scolded the dog.

Pooh just gave a doggy smile and licked her. Calista presented her card for the bill, but the receptionist told her it had already been paid. Leo, she realized. She still didn't understand why he hadn't just thrown her out. After all, he had all the cards since she'd told him the real reason she'd married him.

Her stomach twisted with a strange combination of guilt and loss as she drove to Leo's country home. She spent the day administering medication and TLC to Pooh and wondering what Leo would decide about their marriage. By nightfall, she felt more alone than ever. She took solace in Pooh's presence then went to bed for another mostly sleepless night.

With no word from Leo, she was stuck in limbo. Did he want to end their marriage? She couldn't imagine him wanting to stay with her. In that case, she needed to start searching the job market. Late the following afternoon, Calista's cell phone rang. The caller ID indicated it was her cousin. "Hi Sharon."

"Calista, I have bad news."

"What is it?" Calista asked, turning away from her laptop.

"Tami's been in an accident," she said, her voice quivering.

"Oh, no," Calista said, her heart jumping into her throat. "Is she okay? Is she in the hospital?"

"We're at the hospital right now. She has a few scrapes

and bruises." Sharon paused and lowered her voice. "She was driving drunk."

Calista closed her eyes and shook her head. Guilt rushed through her. Sharon had warned her that Tami had been having trouble, but Calista had buried her head in the sand, hoping that her sister had made a turnaround. "Oh my God."

"I thought she was doing better, but I was obviously wrong. If we could only get her away from that crowd she's been hanging around. And I hate to bring this up, but the ticket and visit to the hospital aren't going to be free."

"No. Of course not. I'll come right away."

"Call me when you get close," Sharon said.

"Will do," she said and turned off her laptop. She grabbed a change of clothes and was torn about telling Leo. Would he even care?

She didn't have time to agonize over it. She typed a text message that would go directly to his BlackBerry then headed downstairs to seek out Meg. "I've had a family emergency, so I need to leave. I'll probably be gone overnight."

Meg's forehead wrinkled in concern. "I'm so sorry."

"Thank you. Could you please watch Pooh while I'm gone?"

"Of course," she said. "I like having the little troublemaker around."

Calista got into her car and pulled out of the driveway. Two minutes later, her phone rang. She picked up. "Hello?"

"It's Leo," he said.

Her heart hammered in her chest at the sound of his voice. "Hi," she said.

"I got your message. What happened? Is Tami hurt?"

A knot formed in her throat. "Not very much physically hurt, but she's done some damage. She was driving my cousin's car and ran into a traffic sign. Unfortunately she was also drunk."

Leo swore.

"Yes," she said in agreement. "Sharon had said she was hanging around a bad crowd, and she'd thought the problem was solved by giving Tami an earlier curfew. I guess now we know that didn't work." She squeezed the steering wheel. "I'm worried about her."

Silence followed. "Maybe you should bring her to the house," he said.

Surprised, Calista blinked. "Uh," she said and cleared her throat. "I wasn't sure *I* should expect to stay at your house."

"I never told you to leave," he said.

"No, but you left," she said. "And I can't blame you after I told you—"

"We'll talk about that later. For now, you need to concentrate on Tami. If you bring her here to stay for a while, she'll have a chance to leave her mistakes in the past and refocus."

"Why would you offer your house to my sister?"

"There may have been a time when I shirked responsibility, but not now," he said in a rock-hard tone.

"You're sure?" she asked, fighting a combination of shock and relief.

"I wouldn't have said it if I weren't. Keep me updated," he said.

"Okay," she said. "Leo, thank—"

"Don't," he cut in. "Drive safely."

* * *

The following evening after Calista helped Tami get settled into a bedroom, Leo sipped a glass of whiskey in his suite as he waited for her. His pride had been stung when he'd learned she'd tricked him for money. After he'd taken time to cool down, however, he could only blame Calista so much. So far, she'd been reluctant to spend a dime of his money. He'd noticed she still paid her own bills from her own checking account. Another woman would have gone hog wild, buying everything in sight.

He also felt somewhat responsible for Calista and her sisters' predicament. He felt more than a twinge of guilt despite the fact that Calista's father had been weak. Like many fools, he'd believed what he wanted to believe. A man like that, with a devoted wife and children, didn't understand what he had.

The bedroom door opened and Calista appeared. She met his gaze solemnly. "Hi."

"Hi,' he said and waved to the chair beside him. "Have a seat."

She walked to the chair and sank into it. A glass of white wine sat on the table waiting for her. She took a sip then set it down. She looked tired, he noted.

"How is Tami?" he asked.

"She's trying to be tough, but she took a stuffed animal to bed with her," she said.

His lips twitched in humor. "Has she said anything?"

"Not much, and that's unusual. She did say she was sorry," she said.

"That's a good start. Realizing you did something wrong is the beginning of being different," he said and took another sip of whiskey. "I should know."

She met his gaze again. "Is that how it happened for you?"

"My so-called adoptive father beat me. He also threatened to beat my adoptive mother. He was manipulative. He trained me to lie, play games and exploit."

She bit her lip. "But you're not like that anymore, are you?"

He shrugged. "Everyone can be manipulative," he said and shot her a pointed look.

She glanced downward. "I can't say I'm innocent in that regard."

"You had good reasons," he said. "I accept that. In a way, I did, too. I was trying to survive. I don't like to be lied to."

"Most of us don't," she said, looking up at him. "Why haven't you kicked me out?"

"Aside from the fact that I still want you," he said and damned if he totally understood why. "It's the right thing to do. Even though my father set up the scheme to trick your father, I benefited from it. You suffered. Your father believed what he wanted to believe instead of the truth."

"He was a good man," she said.

"He may have been a good man, but he was flawed."

"That's a cruel thing to say," she said, her voice choking up.

"It's true."

She glanced away and a faint smile lifted her lips. "He knew how to make us laugh."

"Keep that memory," he told her, wishing he had some of the same kinds of memories.

"What do we do now?" she asked.

"What do you want to do?" he countered.

She fiddled with the stem of her wineglass. "I thought

for sure you'd hate me once I told you I married you to get support for my sisters."

"Do you really think I'm surprised that a woman would marry me for my money?" he asked.

"It's not totally like that," she said, shooting him a look of chagrin.

"Then explain to me how it is," he said, leaning back in his chair.

"I was only going to marry you for six months," she said.

"Ah," he said. "That clause in the prenup."

"Yes, I know it's shameful, but I didn't know how else to provide for Tami and Tina."

"Why didn't you just snag another wealthy man?" he asked. "The first one to come along?"

"Because it didn't seem right," she said. "At least, this way, you were partly responsible for my sisters becoming orphans. I told myself it was a six-month assignment, but the trouble was…" She trailed off and glanced away.

"The trouble was what?" he prompted.

"The trouble was that I liked you," she said with a fierce frown. "And in bed—" She shook her head. "Then you were wonderful about Pooh." She looked perplexed. "And now you're being wonderful about Tami."

He chuckled at her confusion. "Does this mean you want me to go back to your version of Satan?"

She looked at him for a long moment and shook her head. "No," she said softly.

Her expression made his gut knot. He didn't understand it and he sure as hell didn't like it, but he wouldn't ignore it. "You haven't said what you want," he said.

She took a deep breath. "I don't know. I didn't expect you to be like you are. In another situation, I wish you and my father had never met. I wish you and I could have met with no ugly history between us."

"Then let's do that," he said.

She swung her head upward to gape at him. "How?"

"Fresh start. Allow me to introduce myself." He leaned across the table and extended his hand. "I'm Leonardo Grant, your husband."

She stared at his hand for a long moment and paused. She met his gaze. "Hello, Leonardo Grant. I'm Calista French Grant, your wife," she said and slid her hand inside his.

He felt a rocking sense of possession that soared through his blood. "I'm going to want more than six months."

Her eyelids dipped, shielding her expression from him. "Okay."

He stood and tugged her from her chair and pulled her against him. "Starting tonight."

Two mornings later, Leo did his work from his home office. Calista took Pooh in for a checkup and he'd agreed to hang around until she returned. He asked Meg to tell him if and when Tami awakened. Midmorning, his housekeeper tapped at his door.

"She's up, sir," Meg said.

"Thanks. I'll be in the kitchen in a moment." He put his laptop on standby and walked into the kitchen where Tami sat at the bar looking lost.

"Good morning," he said.

She glanced up at him. "Good morning," she returned in a polite but flat tone.

"What do you have planned for today?"

"What can I do? I have no cell phone, no friends," she said.

"You didn't have real friends before," he said.

She crossed her arms over her chest. "You sound like Calista."

"There are worse places, you know," he said, sitting on the stool next to her. "The ghetto, jail."

"Not that you would know," she said.

"Actually I know more than most people would want to know about the ghetto," he said then shrugged. "Did Calista mention that we have horses here?"

"Yes, but I've never ridden."

"Want to learn?" he asked. "Or are you afraid?"

"I'm not afraid," she said. "But who could teach me?"

"That can be arranged," he said. "If you're interested."

"Okay. I'm interested," she said. "Please," she added as if she'd just remembered her manners.

"You have no idea how lucky you are that Calista loves you as much as she does," he told her. "You would be foolish to take that for granted."

Tami's lower lip trembled. "I let her down."

"Yes, you did," he said. "But you still have the opportunity to make her and everyone else who cares about you proud. Including yourself. So why don't you stop pouting and get on with it?"

"How can I? I have no phone, no car," she said.

"Prove you can make good choices. Take an online course and ace it," he said.

"She won't let me near the computer," she said.

"ETR," he said.

Tami frowned. "ETR?" she echoed.

"Earn the right," he said.

"How do I do that?"

"Ask Calista what you can do to help," he said. "What are your favorite pancakes?"

"Blueberry," she said.

"Meg," he called. "Can you please get Miss French some blueberry pancakes?" He walked away to let Tami think about what he'd said. Something told him she would go horseback riding today.

Leo left for a business trip and checked in with Calista several times. He arrived back in town late on Thursday night and headed directly for the shower. After drying off, he went to bed, inhaling her sweet scent as he lifted the covers. In the darkness, he saw the outline of her body and heard her even breathing. He craved the feeling of her naked body against his.

She was asleep, damn it. He would be a caveman to wake her. Closing his eyes, he inhaled deeply. Her scent wafted through him, torturing him.

Suddenly he felt her move and her hand was on his chest. "How did you talk her into horseback riding?" she asked, her breath sliding over his neck.

"I planted the idea," he said.

"Hmm," she said and slid her lips against his jaw. "And the online course?"

"I may have mentioned it," he said.

"I missed you," she whispered.

His heart hammered against his rib cage. "Show me," he told her.

Ten

Calista was relieved that Tami settled into a routine so quickly. Leo had suggested that Tami spend a semester at a local junior college before going away to school. Although Tami was disappointed, she seemed to understand.

Calista's cell phone rang and she glanced at the caller ID, unfamiliar with the number. "Hello?"

"Hi, this is your rock star P.I.," Rob said.

Calista's stomach twisted. "Hi Rob. Thank you for all the information you've sent me. I think I've learned as much as I need to at the moment, so I'll just send you a check."

"Whoa," he said. "You're not blowing me off, are you? Because you should know I've got some amazing new info. It's hot."

"What is it?" she asked reluctantly.

He laughed. "I'm not going to hand it over that easily."

Calista frowned. "What do you mean?"

"I mean now you're in a position to pay me what I deserve, and for this info, I deserve a lot."

Her stomach sank. "I really don't think I need any more information, but what were you planning to charge?"

He named a figure that took her breath away.

"You're crazy," she said. "I don't have that kind of money."

"Give me a break. You're married to the wealthiest man in Philly," he said, his voice full of cynicism.

"That doesn't mean I write checks off his accounts," she said.

Rob paused. "Oh. I wondered if he might tighten the leash on your spending habits after he walked in on you and me."

"Leo doesn't have a leash on my spending, and there's nothing going on between you and me. There never has been."

"If that's true, then you better find a way to write the check for this info, because if you don't want it, I'm going to sell it to the highest bidder and your sugar daddy may not like the way it turns out."

"Are you blackmailing me?" she demanded.

"No, just trying to get my pay. You have my number. Call me if you're interested, but don't wait too long," he said and hung up.

Calista stared at the phone, feeling sick to her stomach. Too upset to sit, she rose to her feet and paced. What did Rob know? He'd said it was *hot*. Would the information ruin Leo? She felt a knot of distress form inside her. She was regretting asking for Rob's help in the first place. She'd thought Rob would at least keep everything he learned confidential. She'd thought he would be ethical.

Ethical. The word hit her in the face. Why should she expect anyone in this situation to be ethical when she couldn't claim the same? Sighing, she shook her head. She was going to have to do something about this. She didn't know how, but she had to do something.

That night after she watched a movie with Tami, Calista joined Leo for a glass of wine and mustered her nerve. "I haven't mentioned this, but there are some checks I need to write and now that I'm not working..."

"Oh," he said with a careless shrug. "I set up an account for you before we got married. I've made a deposit, but my accountant can also add funds. I would have given you the checkbook before, but you were so adamant about not spending my money. You have tuition payments for Tina, don't you?"

She nodded, wondering if he still felt that was a sore spot.

"No problem," he said. "Anything else on your mind?"

She looked away. "Maybe."

"What?"

"This is awkward."

"What?" he asked.

"Back when you partnered with your father on his schemes, did you do any of that after you turned eighteen?" she asked.

"No," he said, his jaw tightening. "I ran away. I like to think my youth should excuse me, but I understood what I was doing, and I hated myself for it."

"But you've turned yourself around. Look at what you've become," she said.

"What's that?" he asked. "How would you describe what I've become?"

"You've become a man," she said. "You take responsibility for your choices. You're vibrant and intelligent, and you may not think it, but you have heart."

He shot her a sympathetic look. "I wouldn't count on that last one too much."

Disappointed and frustrated, she frowned. "You do. Look at what you've done for Tami."

"Some would say that's just payback," he said.

"Then what about our marriage?" she asked. "You want to stick with it. That says something about you."

"We made a deal, a bargain." He slid his hand under her chin. "I care for you. I want you. I'll take care of you. But don't expect the fairy tale. I think you and I both know better than that. Remember it and you'll be happier."

His ability to detach himself made something inside her freeze with fear. Was he truly incapable of emotion? Of love? Why did it matter? she asked herself. He was taking care of the financial end of things. That was all she'd ever wanted. Right?

Calista stared at him, suddenly slapped with the knowledge that her feelings for Leo ran deeper than she'd ever anticipated. And it hurt that he clearly didn't return her feelings.

"Calista?" he said, lifting his eyebrows. "You agree with what I've said, don't you?"

She bit the inside of her lip. "I see your point."

"Hedging," he said.

She played the girl card. "Do you really want to get into

a messy emotional argument with a female late at night?" she challenged with a smile.

"God, no," he said with a look of pure horror.

"Then let's go to bed," she said and told herself she would think about what he'd said some other time.

The next morning, she gave Rob a call. "I'd like to meet with you," she said.

"You have a check?" he asked.

"Yes, but you'll have to sign an agreement that you won't give any of the information you've discovered about my father or Leo to anyone else," she said firmly.

"Those are high demands. I could get some nice cash if I sold this to a tabloid," he said.

"Or not," she said. "Leo keeps a low profile. He's not a Hollywood star or a jet-setter, therefore, you could be taking the risk of getting much less. Or nothing."

"Oooh," he said. "Somebody grew kahunas. Okay, meet me at Liberty Bar at seven."

"No," she said. "I've got the check. We'll meet at three o'clock."

"No can do at three o'clock," he said. "I've got another job. Make it five-thirty and I can swing it."

Calista hated the timing, but she needed to get this taken care of immediately. "Okay. Don't be late," she said and hung up.

Calista visited the bar where she was supposed to meet Rob and waited. Thirty minutes passed and he finally showed up. "Where have you been?" she demanded.

"I got hung up," he said. "Where's the check?"

"Where's the information?" she retorted.

"You're getting tough, girl," he said and pulled out a manila envelope. "Check first."

"Signature first," she said and presented a legal document and copies for him to sign.

Rob read it and whistled. "You covered all the bases. Name changes and everything."

"If you want the money, sign it," she said.

He signed three copies of the document. "I don't suppose you'll give me a recommendation to your wealthy friends," he said.

"I don't like it that you changed the charge midstream," she said.

"That was only done after I realized I didn't have a shot at you," he said.

Calista felt nervous with each passing second. She had the odd feeling that someone was watching her, but she didn't know who. "Here's the check," she said.

Rob passed the folder to her and she stood. He followed and kissed her cheek. She drew back and frowned.

"You can't blame me. I came this close to a Philly Princess," he said, lifting his thumb and forefinger, pressing them together.

"You flatter yourself," she said and walked away. She got into her car and drove to Leo's house, the folder sitting beside her, nearly burning a hole in the passenger seat. It was dark when she pulled into the garage, and she winced when she saw Leo's car already parked in its regular spot.

Praying he wouldn't have noticed, she grabbed the folder and walked inside. The house was silent. George stepped into the hallway. "Mrs. Grant, where have you been?"

She didn't like his suspicious tone, or was it her imagination? "Out," she said. "And you?"

He raised his eyebrows in surprise. "Mr. Grant is looking for you."

"Where is he?" she asked.

"In your suite."

"Thank you," she said.

Her stomach clenched in knots, she climbed the stairs to their bedroom suite. She opened the door and found Leo facing the window, his hands on his hips. "Where have you been?"

"Out," she said, walking toward him, hating the wall he seemed to have drawn around himself.

He turned and threw some photos on the table beside him. "I see you met with your friend again," he said.

She glanced closer at the photos, seeing the damning visual of Rob kissing her cheek. Humiliation suffused her. "It's not what it looks like."

"Oh, really?" he said in a cold voice. "Then how is it?"

"Are you willing to listen?"

"Why should I?" he asked in a dead voice. "You'll only lie."

Her anger jumped inside her. "Stop it," she said. "You owe me the chance to explain."

"I owe you nothing," he said.

"Fine, then you'll never know what I spent a hundred thousand dollars of your money on. At this point, I don't even know. I just know I made Rob sign an agreement not to share the information."

Leo paused and frowned. "What the hell are you talking about?"

"Rob said he had information about you, but it was big. He told me I had to pay. That's why I asked you about money."

Realization dawned on Leo's face, but he was still cautious. "What information?"

She opened the folder. "Let's find out."

* * *

Leo scanned the report with skepticism. One of his security men had followed Calista and taken photos of her with the P.I. They'd been e-mailed to him and he'd printed them off, ready to throw her out of the house.

Now, he wasn't so sure. Calista's P.I. said his real name was Leonardo Medici and he had three brothers. Both his parents were dead. His father had died in a train accident. He was supposed to have died in the same accident, but an explosion threw him away from the train. He frowned as he read the story. Was it true? Was he the boy who'd survived?

According to the report, a woman had discovered him and taken him home. That was when Clyde had become his so-called adoptive father. That was when the abuse had begun.

"Oh my God," Calista whispered. She looked at him. "You survived a train wreck. Not a car accident."

He shook his head. "We don't know that for sure."

She lifted the written report, which was followed by photos of his brothers. "Look at them. They look just like you," she said. "They're your brothers."

Too stunned to take it all in, he shook his head. "I put my own P.I. on this. Why wasn't he able to find it?"

"Maybe, despite Rob's obnoxiousness, he got lucky and dug in the right place. Leo, this is amazing. Momentuous. You have to call your brothers. They will be so happy you're alive."

"How do you know?" he asked and shook his head. "What am I going to tell them? I had a criminal past and have a fake marriage."

Calista turned pale. "Is that what you really think?" she asked, shaking her head. "I know you don't believe in all the romance, but do you really believe our marriage is fake? I thought we'd both decided we wanted a fresh start. I thought that meant we were building something real."

Leo stood. The news about his family was too overwhelming. He didn't trust it. He didn't trust Calista. He didn't want to count on her. He'd learned he couldn't count on anyone. "What's reality? What's perception? I don't remember these brothers. They're not real to me. Why should I get in touch with them?"

"Because they're your family," she insisted. "And based on this report, they want to find you. Can you imagine how much pain they've experienced thinking you're missing or dead? For all these years," she said.

Leo walked to the window and stared outside. This was what he'd dreamed of for years, but he couldn't go after it. He'd changed from whomever he'd been when they'd known him. And not necessarily for the best.

Calista gently touched his arm. "Leo, I know you had a terrible childhood after the accident, but you've come out of it an amazing person. You've become a man I could fall in love with," she confessed and his gut tightened. "A man I have fallen in love with."

Her admission struck him at his core, but he couldn't accept it. He couldn't believe it. "My money is making life easier for you and your sisters. Don't mistake your gratitude for love, Calista."

He heard her shocked intake of breath and she snatched her hand away from him as if she'd burned it. Remorse surged through him. He hadn't wanted to hurt her, but he couldn't open up to her, especially now. "Calista," he said, turning.

She backed away, shaking her head, tears in her eyes. "No."

"Calista," he said again, moving toward her.

"No, really. Don't say another word," she whispered and ran from the room.

She didn't return to his bed that night and he didn't go looking for her. Leo stared at the ceiling for most of the night. He couldn't believe the P.I.'s report. He had brothers. His mother and father had died. Medici was his real last name. He whispered it. "Medici." It rolled off his tongue with a strange familiarity.

What had happened to his brothers, he wondered. What kind of course had their lives taken? He'd stopped reading the report midway. Unable to tamp down his curiosity, he got up and began to read it. Damien Medici, 35 years old, married, successful CEO of his own business. Rafe Medici, 33 years old, married. One son, another child on the way.

Something inside him twisted at the thought of a nephew.

Leo swore under his breath. He didn't know these people. This wasn't real to him and it never would be. He shoved the report into a drawer and glanced at the clock. Four o'clock in the morning. Screw it. He would go into the office. He couldn't stand being in his own skin at the moment. Work would be his panacea. It always had been.

When Leo arrived home that night, Meg greeted him, but Pooh didn't.

"Welcome home, Mr. Grant. Would you like a cocktail?" she asked.

Leo glanced around, frowning. "Where's the dog?"

"Oh, Mrs. Grant took him with her," she said.

"Excuse me?" he said, his gut tightening.

Meg nodded. "Mrs. Grant left this morning. She said she didn't know when she'd be back." Meg paused. "Shall I tell the chef to prepare your meal?"

He shook his head. "Just a sandwich will do. I'll be in my office." Feeling a sense of dread, he walked to his office. He'd been hard on her last night. Too hard? He wondered if she'd decided not to stay. He punched out the number to her cell phone, but it went straight to voice mail. No message, no note. Where had she gone?

The sense of dread in his gut grew to a large knot. Calista was gone. Tami was gone. Pooh was gone. And Calista wasn't answering her phone. Leo did the math and suspected Calista had left him for good.

The thought made every cell inside him hurt. The sensation shocked him. He hadn't believed he was that vulnerable. But maybe he was.

He swore underneath his breath. Leo had always told himself not to count on people, including Calista. He'd clearly failed. From the first minute he'd seen her, he'd wanted her. Aside from her obvious physical assets, she'd had a charm about her that made him feel warm inside. Just by her presence, she'd made everywhere they were together feel like home.

She'd made him want to open up to things he'd closed himself to in the past. She'd made him want to be the man she needed. The man who would take care of her and her sisters financially. The good man she could count on in an emergency. He'd seduced her and married her, but he couldn't give her what she'd ended up wanting and needing from him. The one thing he hadn't thought he would ever experience. Love. The biggest grifter scheme of all. Even though she'd known about his past, known that he was a con man, she'd made him feel like a real man.

Leo climbed the stairs to his bedroom, dreading entering it again. Once inside, the subtle remnant of the scent of her perfume haunted him. The possibilities he'd felt with her haunted him. He tried to push thoughts of her from his mind, but it was impossible. Images seeped inside him like smoke under the door. He wondered if he would ever be the same again. Did he want to be?

Everywhere he looked, he saw her, heard her laughter, felt her silky skin and warmth. He couldn't stand the memories. He had to get out of here.

George drove him to a hotel in downtown Philadelphia. "Is there something wrong with the penthouse?" he asked.

Only that Calista had been there and he needed to go somewhere she hadn't. It was the only way he could escape his thoughts about her. "No," Leo said, but added nothing.

"Are you meeting someone?" George asked.

Leo frowned at his longtime sparring partner. "God, no. I just need a different environment."

George glanced in the rearview mirror. "When is Mrs. Grant supposed to be back?"

"I don't know. You'll have to ask her," Leo said, staring out the window into the night.

"It's not my place to interfere," George said.

"That's right," Leo said. "It's not."

"But you could go after her," George said. "If you want her."

Leo narrowed his eyes, feeling as if his insides were being torn apart. He knew. He sensed it deep inside him. He'd smashed her overtures repeatedly. "It's too late."

* * *

Two days later, Leo felt like death warmed over. He hadn't slept more than a couple hours each night. Taunted by need for Calista and unanswered questions about his past family, he'd found no rest or peace. Staying at the hotel hadn't helped one damn bit. Now he just imagined he could smell her and hear her voice.

He cloistered himself in his office. He must have looked frightening. Even his assistant appeared reluctant to approach him. He received an odd text. Mr. Grant, your housekeeper called. There is a problem at your home in the country that needs to be addressed immediately.

Leo picked up his phone and paged his assistant. "I'm busy. What kind of problem?" Leo asked.

"I'm not certain sir. I only know she sounded upset when she called, sir," his assistant said.

Leo heard an odd nervousness in his assistant's voice. "Call her back and get specific information."

"I've already done that, sir, but there was no answer."

Leo frowned. "What the hell," he muttered.

"I'm very sorry for the interruption, sir. Shall I page George?"

"Yes," Leo said tersely.

His mood, which had already been nasty, deteriorated with each passing mile. As George drove inside the gates to the large home, he spotted a stretch limousine parked in front of his house. "What's going on? Don't bother with the garage. I'm getting to the bottom of this."

Leo strode up the steps to the front door. The house was completely silent. For once, Meg didn't greet him. He walked four steps into the foyer and Calista appeared.

Leo felt as if he were viewing an apparition. God knew,

he'd seen her in his dreams and mind every other minute during the last few days. "What are you doing here?"

She met his gaze and took a deep breath. "I'm about to piss you off."

Confusion rushed through him. The apparition spoke. "What are you talking about?"

"You know the old saying, If Mohammed won't come to the mountain, then the mountain must come to Mohammed?"

"Yes," he said, starting to realize that she wasn't a figment of his imagination. "Where have you been? Why did you leave?"

"I had to. I had to do it. If I really loved you, there was no other choice."

He felt as if she'd just punched him. "You're making no sense. Are you here to stay or not?"

"You might be throwing me out in a few minutes," she muttered. "I took Tami and Pooh to my cousin's house then flew to Atlanta to visit one of your brothers. They're waiting to meet you in the living room."

His heart stopped and his jaw dropped. "All of them?"

She gave a shaky laugh. "Once they heard you were alive, nothing would have stopped them." Her eyes filled with emotion. "You may not think you need them, but you do. And for them, you're the missing link."

Leo found that difficult to believe, but he couldn't resist the love shining from Calista's gaze. She'd made this trip out of love for him even though he'd brushed her hopes aside. How had he gotten so lucky? How had he managed to find the one woman who would see beyond his detachment with the world and burrow her way into his heart? Looking at her, he felt the magic of possibility again. She made him feel as if he really was better than his past.

"Come here," he said, staring at her in wonder. "You are the biggest miracle of my life. Never leave me again."

Calista's eyes filled with tears. "Oh, Leo, don't say that if you don't mean it."

"I do. I never thought I could love a woman like I love you."

Her mouth dropped open in breathless surprise.

"Yes," he said. "I love you."

She let out a sob of relief and lifted her hand to touch his face. "I knew when I did this that you might never forgive me, but I had to take the chance. I realize this might be difficult, but if you want me with you, I'll stay."

"Forever," he said. "All I want is forever."

She closed her eyes then opened them again. "You've got me."

He pressed his mouth against hers, needing to seal their promises to each other. Then he pulled back. "Time for me to meet my family," he said and he walked with Calista into the living room.

Three men with hair and eyes that matched his looked at him and in the dark, shadowy edges of his mind, a visual flashed of all of them racing toward the dinner table. He could almost smell the scent of spices, meat, sausage, tomatoes and fresh pasta.

"I don't have any concrete memories," he said, feeling compelled to break the news right away.

"They already know that," Calista said and stepped away from him.

One stepped forward. Leo remembered him from the P.I. report. "We can fill you in," he said and offered his hand. "Rafe," he added.

"I know," Leo said. "I read the report. I think I've memorized it." He glanced up. "Damien and Michael." He hesitated, an unbelievable whirlpool of feelings welling inside him. "My past isn't pretty."

"We don't care," Damien said, extending his hand. "We're just glad you survived."

Leo felt strange emotion form a knot in his throat as Michael walked toward him. There was turbulence in his eyes. "You need to know. You were on that train instead of me. If I hadn't gotten into trouble, it would have been me on that train. I wished for it so many times."

It struck Leo that he wasn't the only one carrying around a load of guilt. It also struck him that fate had dealt a hand in his life, bad and good. "Fate's a tricky witch," he realized and glanced at his brothers and Calista. "I can't be sorry for what I've gone through if this is what I've gotten in the end."

Epilogue

On New Year's Eve, the Medici brothers, *all* the Medici brothers, gathered at Michael's house in Grand Cayman to ring in the new year together. Although they had kept in touch since their first meeting, this was the first time they'd been able to come together due to their busy schedules. Everyone was happy to escape the winter blahs and relax at the Caribbean island. Calista sat next to Leo, happily taking in the hustle and bustle of the celebration.

Rafe juggled playing with his son, Joel, and holding his new baby daughter, Angelica. His wife, Nicole, took Angelica from his arms. "Time for her nap. You can't hold her all the time."

"If she didn't look like a miniature version of you, it wouldn't be a problem," he growled, taking his wife's lips in a quick kiss.

"Rafe is going to end up with twelve kids. He's a natural father," Damien said with a knowing glance.

Nicole shot him a look of horror. "I think twelve is tipping the scales. He'll be happy to enjoy some nieces and nephews." She smiled at Damien's wife, Emma, who was six months pregnant. "Just make sure you get them started changing diapers early on."

Damien looked at Emma with a skeptical raised eyebrow. "Do you really think you can talk me into changing diapers?"

Emma lifted his hand to her baby bump. "You tell me."

Damien's hard gaze softened and anyone could see he would do anything for his wife, including changing diapers.

Michael, sitting next to Leo, lifted a beer. "Cheers to Damien and Rafe for taking on father duty. I'll let you take the lead." He patted his wife's leg. "Bella and I are in no rush at all. Right?"

Bella shot him a pained look. "There's something I've been meaning to tell you."

Michael looked at her in confusion. "What?" he asked.

Silence fell over the tiled porch.

Michael's lovely wife shot him a nervous look. "You know how we were afraid I'd gotten a stomach flu?"

Michael set down his beer. "Yes, are you okay? Is it something more serious?"

"Well, my condition lasts about nine months and you might need to bone up on changing diapers, too. I'm pregnant. Is that okay?"

Michael's color drained from his face. "You're pregnant. How did that happen?"

"The usual way, sweetie. You remember that time in the limo when we left the opera early…."

"Oh, yeah," he said, realization crossing his face. Still stunned, he stared at her. "We're gonna have a baby?"

She nodded. "Are you upset?"

He shook his head and pulled her into his arms. "How could I be? You and I made this together."

Damien chuckled. "To Michael, uncle and father-to-be," he said, lifting his beer.

Everyone lifted their drinks. "Hear, hear," they chorused.

Lifting her own glass of lemonade, Calista felt a twist in her stomach. She wondered when she should tell Leo.

"Looks like it's in the water," Leo muttered to her as the group began to chatter with excitement. "We'd better be careful."

Calista mustered her courage. "I think it may be a little late for that," she whispered.

Leo swung his head around to stare at her. "Excuse me?"

"I wasn't really sure until day before yesterday," she said.

"Why didn't you tell me?" he asked in a low voice.

"I couldn't figure out the best time."

"Are you sure?"

Calista was feeling more nervous with each passing moment. "I took three at-home pregnancy tests and was also tested at the doctor."

"Do you want this?" he asked, his gaze intent and so focused on her they may as well have been the only ones around for miles.

"I do," she confessed. "I can't think of anything better

than making a new life with the amazing man I love more than anything."

He took her hand and this time his hand trembled. "You keep making me happier than I've ever dreamed I could be."

Her heart expanded in her chest so much it hurt. "You keep doing the same to me." She leaned forward and pressed her lips against his. "Don't stop."

"Never," he promised.

"Hey, Leo, take a break from your lovefest with your wife," Rafe said. "Do you shoot pool?"

"Yeah, I do," he said. "But I think we may need another round of drinks. Calista and I are going to have a baby." He shot Michael a stunned look. "Looks like you and I may be on the same daddy schedule."

Michael gave a half smile and moved toward him, extending his hand. Leo rose and shook his brother's hand. "This is one trip we can finally take together."

"To Leo and Calista," Damien said.

"Hear, hear," the families chorused.

"And to Aunt Emilia for pictures and encouragement," Michael said.

Leo toasted the aunt he'd met through his brothers' letters and photographs then pulled Calista against him. "Thank you for giving me all this," he said. "But mostly for giving me you."

* * * * *

*Harlequin offers a romance for every mood!
See below for a sneak peek
from our paranormal romance line,
Silhouette® Nocturne™.
Enjoy a preview of REUNION by USA TODAY
bestselling author Lindsay McKenna.*

Aella closed her eyes and sensed a distinct shift, like movement from the world around her to the unseen world.

She opened her eyes. And had a slight shock at the man standing ten feet away. He wasn't just any man. Her heart leaped and pounded. He reminded her of a fierce warrior from an ancient civilization. Incan? She wasn't sure but she felt his deep power and masculinity.

I'm Aella. Are you the guardian of this sacred site? she asked, hoping her telepathy was strong.

Fox's entire body soared with joy. Fox struggled to put his personal pleasure aside.

Greetings, Aella. I'm the assistant guardian to this sacred area. You may call me Fox. How can I be of service to you, Aella? he asked.

I'm searching for a green sphere. A legend says that the Emperor Pachacuti had seven emerald spheres created for the Emerald Key necklace. He had seven of his priestesses and priests travel the world to hide these spheres from evil forces. It is said that when all seven spheres are found, restrung and worn, that Light will return to the Earth. The fourth sphere is here, at your sacred site. Are you aware of it? Aella held her breath. She loved looking at him, especially his sensual mouth. The desire to kiss him came out of nowhere.

Fox was stunned by the request. *I know of the Emerald Key necklace because I served the emperor at the time it was created. However, I did not realize that one of the spheres is here.*

Aella felt sad. Why? Every time she looked at Fox, her heart felt as if it would tear out of her chest. *May I stay in touch with you as I work with this site?* she asked.

Of course. Fox wanted nothing more than to be here with her. To absorb her ephemeral beauty and hear her speak once more.

Aella's spirit lifted. What *was* this strange connection between them? Her curiosity was strong, but she had more pressing matters. In the next few days, Aella knew her life would change forever. How, she had no idea....

Look for REUNION
by USA TODAY *bestselling author*
Lindsay McKenna,
available April 2010, only from
Silhouette® Nocturne™.

HARLEQUIN® Romance®

ROMANCE, RIVALRY
AND A FAMILY REUNITED

THE BRIDES of BELLA ROSA

William Valentine and his beloved wife, Lucia, live
a beautiful life together, but when his former love Rosa
and the secret family they had together resurface,
an instant rivalry is formed. Can these families
get through the past and come together as one?

*Step into the world of Bella Rosa
beginning this April with*

Beauty and the Reclusive Prince
by
RAYE MORGAN

Eight volumes to collect and treasure!

HARLEQUIN®

INTRIGUE®

WILL THIS REUNITED FAMILY
BE STRONG ENOUGH TO EXPOSE
A LURKING KILLER?

FIND OUT IN THIS ALL-NEW
THRILLING TRILOGY FROM TOP
HARLEQUIN INTRIGUE AUTHOR

B.J. DANIELS

WHITEHORSE
MONTANA

Winchester Ranch

GUN-SHY BRIDE—*April 2010*

HITCHED—*May 2010*

TWELVE-GAUGE GUARDIAN—
June 2010

Silhouette®

SPECIAL EDITION

**INTRODUCING A BRAND-NEW MINISERIES
FROM *USA TODAY* BESTSELLING AUTHOR**

KASEY MICHAELS

SECOND-CHANCE
BRIDAL

At twenty-eight, widowed single mother
Elizabeth Carstairs thinks she's left love behind
forever....until she meets Will Hollingsbrook.
Her sons' new baseball coach is the handsomest
man she's ever seen—and the more time they
spend together, the more undeniable the
connection between them. But can Elizabeth
leave the past behind and open her heart to
a second chance at love?

FIND OUT IN

SUDDENLY A BRIDE

*Available in April
wherever books are sold.*

Visit Silhouette Books at www.eHarlequin.com

SSE65517

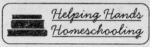

2 Stories in 1

HER MEDITERRANEAN PLAYBOY

Sexy and dangerous—he wants you in his bed!

The sky is blue, the azure sea is crashing
against the golden sand and the sun is hot.

The conditions are perfect for
a scorching Mediterranean seduction
from two irresistible untamed playboys!

Indulge your senses with these two delicious stories

A MISTRESS AT THE ITALIAN'S COMMAND
by Melanie Milburne

ITALIAN BOSS, HOUSEKEEPER MISTRESS
by Kate Hewitt

Available April 2010 from Harlequin Presents!

www.eHarlequin.com

HP12910

Stay up-to-date on all your romance-reading news with the brand-new Harlequin *Inside Romance!*

The Harlequin *Inside Romance* is a **FREE** quarterly newsletter highlighting our upcoming series releases and promotions!

Click on the *Inside Romance* link on the front page of www.eHarlequin.com or e-mail us at InsideRomance@Harlequin.ca to sign up to receive your FREE newsletter today!

You can also subscribe by writing to us at: HARLEQUIN BOOKS
Attention: Customer Service Department
P.O. Box 9057, Buffalo, NY 14269-9057

Please allow 4-6 weeks for delivery of the first issue by mail.

IRNBPAQ309

REQUEST YOUR FREE BOOKS!

2 FREE NOVELS PLUS 2 FREE GIFTS!

Silhouette Desire®

Passionate, Powerful, Provocative!

YES! Please send me 2 FREE Silhouette Desire® novels and my 2 FREE gifts (gifts are worth about $10). After receiving them, if I don't wish to receive any more books, I can return the shipping statement marked "cancel." If I don't cancel, I will receive 6 brand-new novels every month and be billed just $4.05 per book in the U.S. or $4.74 per book in Canada. That's a saving of almost 15% off the cover price! It's quite a bargain! Shipping and handling is just 50¢ per book in the U.S. and 75¢ per book in Canada.* I understand that accepting the 2 free books and gifts places me under no obligation to buy anything. I can always return a shipment and cancel at any time. Even if I never buy another book, the two free books and gifts are mine to keep forever.

225 SDN E39X 326 SDN E4AA

Name	(PLEASE PRINT)

Address		Apt. #

City	State/Prov.	Zip/Postal Code

Signature (if under 18, a parent or guardian must sign)

Mail to the **Silhouette Reader Service:**
IN U.S.A.: P.O. Box 1867, Buffalo, NY 14240-1867
IN CANADA: P.O. Box 609, Fort Erie, Ontario L2A 5X3

Not valid for current subscribers to Silhouette Desire books.

Want to try two free books from another line?
Call 1-800-873-8635 or visit www.morefreebooks.com.

* Terms and prices subject to change without notice. Prices do not include applicable taxes. N.Y. residents add applicable sales tax. Canadian residents will be charged applicable provincial taxes and GST. Offer not valid in Quebec. This offer is limited to one order per household. All orders subject to approval. Credit or debit balances in a customer's account(s) may be offset by any other outstanding balance owed by or to the customer. Please allow 4 to 6 weeks for delivery. Offer available while quantities last.

Your Privacy: Silhouette Books is committed to protecting your privacy. Our Privacy Policy is available online at www.eHarlequin.com or upon request from the Reader Service. From time to time we make our lists of customers available to reputable third parties who may have a product or service of interest to you. If you would prefer we not share your name and address, please check here. ☐

Help us get it right—We strive for accurate, respectful and relevant communications. To clarify or modify your communication preferences, visit us at www.ReaderService.com/consumerschoice.

SDES10